D1520141

TRACER

The Zoo Crew Series, Book 3

DUSTIN STEVENS

"Montana seems to me to be what a small boy would think Texas is like from hearing Texans."
-John Steinbeck

PROLOGUE

Brand.

Derived from an Old Norse language word meaning *to burn*.

Dating back thousands of years, the term has referred to the practice of marking one's products with a particular insignia.

It can be a name. A design. A symbol. Most anything a producer wants it to be.

The most important thing is that it demarcates Product A from Product B.

Even in an intangible form, a brand can be the most valuable asset a producer possesses. Without it, there is no marketing. Without marketing, there are no consumers.

Without consumers, there's no point in a product.

Over time, two different types of brands have emerged. The first is those employed by companies, mass corporations that rely on international product recognition to peddle their wares.

Coca-Cola. McDonald's. Apple.

The heavy-hitters, recognized in an instant. Not just logos, but a symbolic construct within the mind. All the information and expectation associated with a product, encapsulated in a single image.

The other type of brand - the one far more relevant in Montana - is the cattle brand.

Again tracing back to the Old Norse root of the word, it means the marking of one's product by burning.

When ranching first became a vocation in America, delineating one herd from another was a serious problem. For Samuel Augustus Maverick, famed 19th century Texas cattleman, it was such an issue that his name became synonymous with roaming free.

A maverick.

To fix this problem, ranchers began marking their cattle. Branding them.

Taking an iron rod with a basic design. Heating it in a fire. Pressing it against a cow's hide.

The impending scar was prominent enough that a cowboy could differentiate one herd from another each year at roundup.

This worked well for a while, but it didn't take long for roughnecks to start gaming the system. Running irons. Changing brands to their own marking.

Laws were enacted calling for brands to be filed and registered. Cattle on drives were stopped for inspection. A bill of sale was required outlining every animal purchased.

Over time, the reliance on branding shifted. No longer was it used to cover open-range animals. Instead, it became used as the proof of ownership standard for lost or stolen cattle.

With the advent of technology, various other forms of identification came to the surface. Lip or ear tattoos. Earmarking. Tagging. Even microchipping.

At the end of the day though, the goal is always to identify one's product from another's.

To brand them.

To a rancher, just like any other corporation, the brand is their livelihood.

It is something to be protected at all costs. To be fought for, ensuring a way of life.

Most of the time, that fighting is done within a court of law, perhaps even in an agricultural hearing.

Then again, sometimes it isn't

CHAPTER ONE

Pissed.

Not miffed. Not worked up.

Not even angry.

Flat out pissed.

The interior of the truck was dark, silent, cold, as Lukas Webb sat behind the wheel. His pulse hammered through his temples. His breath pushed out in loud bursts through his nose.

In the Army, he'd been taught exercises for this type of moment. Methods of breathing. Ways of detaching his active mind and taking himself far away. Soothing his nerves so he could focus on the task at hand.

That was easy, though.

That involved staring through a scope at a man he'd never met. Bearing down on someone that had never wronged him personally.

Or even worse, wronged his family.

Lukas thought for a moment about the exercises. About the way his spotter Rick Bailey had always told him to go through them before taking a shot.

To calm the nerves. Clear the mind.

Just as fast, the thought passed.

He didn't need sharp eyes or a steady hand for what he was about to do. All he needed was enough wherewithal to make sure he didn't go off script.

Turn things uglier than they already were.

Condensation collected on the windows as Lukas remained in the truck, stewing. In his mind, he could still see the smug face of the bastard as he sat at the head of the table. As he sneered and told Lukas there wasn't enough time for him to speak.

The thought made his blood run hot.

It was all Lukas could do to turn around and walk back out into the night instead of going straight down the aisle and ripping him apart.

Despite the temperature inside the truck, Lukas could feel a film of sweat on his skin. He ran a thumb across his brow, feeling the sting as droplets reached his eyes.

He could taste salt on his upper lip.

Without turning in the front seat, Lukas raised his right hand and hefted down the 30.06 from the window behind him. It slid easily from its perch in the top slot of the gun rack, the implement familiar in his hands.

Rotating his arm at the wrist, he laid the weapon across his lap and stared down at it. The cherry stock gleamed, catching a bit of the light from the security post outside.

The tips of Lukas' fingers grazed along the woodwork, recalling the dozen mule deer he'd slain with it.

Hunting.

A most noble cause for such a fine weapon. Nothing like what he was about to do.

Pressing his lips tight, Lukas reached down into the passenger foot well. Took up a small cardboard box of ammunition.

He fished in and snagged a pair of shells, their red tips visible in the cab.

Lukas rubbed the pad of his index finger against the side of his nose. Streaked the resulting oil along the shells. Inserted them one at a time into the gun.

Locked them into place with the distinct clang of metal on metal.

Practiced hands worked the bolt-action lever, positioning the cartridges.

Lukas gripped the weapon and stared through the front windshield of his truck. Gaze focused through the small hole that wasn't fogged over. Attention aimed on the front door.

Inside, there were over 50 people, some women and children.

There was no doubt what he was about to do would scare the hell out of many of them.

It didn't matter, though. They were in no real danger.

There was only one target tonight. At such a close range, there was no way he would miss.

With a heavy breath, Lukas wrenched the door open. Heard the springs groan in protest, frozen metal scraping against itself.

Cold air swirled around him as he stepped outside. Felt the rims of his nostrils draw tight. Heard his boots crunch on the hardened ground as he walked.

The stock of the rifle he kept gripped in his right hand, the barrel in his left.

With each step, his heart rate rose a bit more. His breathing gained speed.

This was not the first time he'd ever fired in a crowded place. Far from it. Still, it was the first time he's ever done so on American soil.

First time he'd ever done it at home.

Keeping his left hand wrapped around the barrel, he reached out and jerked the front door wide with his right. A burst of hot air mussed the hair atop his head as he stepped through the buffer zone.

Heard the overhead fans pushing stale air down at him.

The second door opened with a small squeal, his right hand finding the stock of the rifle again the moment he passed through.

Ahead of him, the door to the meeting hall stood agape, the entire council seated in a row at the head of the room. He could see his target sitting front and center, a cocksure smile on his face.

With determined strides Lukas covered the gap, bursting in before anyone even knew he was there. Stopping just inside the door, he raised the gun to his shoulder.

The face of his target crinkled into a look of horror as he saw Lukas standing with the rifle.

A moment later, those fanned out to either side of him did the same.

A single scream erupted from a woman at the table as Lukas sighted in. The sound had no effect on him, his breathing leveling out as his finger found the trigger and squeezed.

The big gun bucked against his shoulder with a mighty kick. Over 20 pounds of recoil concentrated against his rotator cuff. A moment later came the thunderous sound, a cannon shot reverberating off the walls of the enclosed space.

The entire room flashed red.

Lukas didn't notice as he shifted his aim two inches to the left.

Fired again.

CHAPTER TWO

Boredom.

Extreme, mind-numbing, soul-crushing, boredom.

The feeling gripped every fiber of Hank McIlvaine's being as he sat in the back of the meeting room. Ran his gaze over the crowd time and time again. Sat alert for an enemy that was never coming.

McIlvaine had been on the payroll for almost two months now. A stint that started just before Halloween, would end sometime after Christmas.

He hoped.

The job as described was an easy one. Provide personal security and assistance to a cattle baron. Get off the oil rigs. Out of Eastern Montana, where the landscape and the women were both wind-blown and brittle dry.

Return to his old stomping grounds in the western half of the state. Back to hitting the bars in Hamilton, catching football games on the weekend in Missoula.

In return for getting his life back, all he had to do was ride shotgun for the old fart. Provide backup for a Dandy that didn't have the weight in his britches to do things himself. Thought of himself as an old-time maven that was in reality just another rancher.

A big one, but still just a rancher.

McIlvaine barely listened as he was told how much his services would render financially. It didn't matter. The oil life wasn't one for him, even less so with winter fast approaching.

He signed the dotted line just minutes after being approached.

In the months since, his life had slowed to brutal monotony. Accompanying the old man as he drove the perimeter of his ranch. Running background checks on all ranch employees. Making the occasional food run.

Sitting through every long, tedious meeting the old man had. What it was he was waiting for wasn't quite clear, but wait he did anyway.

All the way to the bank every Monday.

Perched in the back corner, McIlvaine made it through the first hour easy enough. He wasn't interested in agriculture or zoning, but he followed along the best he could.

Enough to know whether a potential threat would surface from the room.

For a few brief moments, his radar had pinged hot at the tall blonde man across the room. Ramrod straight and hair shorn tight on the sides, he wore the look of a man fresh out of the military.

McIlvaine recognized it right off, he'd seen it enough times over the years. Even briefly wore it himself a long time ago.

What jumped out at him was the crazed look in the young man's eyes. A look that said he was insulted. Aggrieved. Put upon.

And he would do anything to the man that had inflicted it.

McIlvaine knew that look even better than the first. It was one he still wore quite often.

To his great surprise - and even disappointment - the young man swallowed the look down. Fought back his natural reaction, turned and left the room.

McIlvaine gave it five minutes to make sure the hostility of the moment was gone. Went back to thumbing through his iPhone and checking college football scores.

Trying to drown out the incessant rambling of the meeting around him.

Because of that, the opening of the front door didn't register with him. Nor did the sound of boots against hardwood floor.

It wasn't until he heard the all-too-familiar sound of a bolt-action rifle that he shifted his focus upward. Saw the young man was back, the look in his eyes stronger than before.

McIlvaine's jaw dropped a half inch as he glanced from the man to the front of the room and back again. His hand reached for the Springfield XD Compact .45 holstered beneath his jacket and drew it out as the man fired his first shot.

The world glowed bright crimson as he attempted to raise the gun. Instead of firing, he used it to shield his eyes from the intense light illuminating the room.

The second shot went off much like the first, a mighty echo through the town hall.

Another blinding burst of light.

Eyes squinted against the searing blaze, McIlvaine raised the Springfield. Aimed it in the general direction of the man, little more than a dark shadow in a sanguineous cloud.

Squeezed the trigger once.

Twice.

Until there were no rounds left in the weapon. Nothing but the empty click of a firing pin touching air.

CHAPTER THREE

Last.

The last run of the day.

The last Zoo Crew outing of the year.

The last 10 minutes before retiring to the lodge for breakfast.

Drake Bell and Sage Keuhl were the first two off the ski lift, per usual. Every trip up the mountain they rode together, Drake on the inside to block the wind sweeping in from Hellgate Canyon to the east. Sage hunkered down beside him, pretending not to be using his body as a windbreak.

Both of their snowboards hung down beneath them, clipped in by a single ski boot, the other foot swinging free.

Jumping off a moment later came Ajax and Kade Keuhl, the other half of the Zoo Crew.

They too always rode together, Kade on the inside to block the wind for Ajax. Despite being a 6'4" male and living in Missoula all of his adult life, the cold cut through him with every icy blast.

It was funny the first couple of years.

Now, it just bordered on sad.

"Alright, one last time," Drake said as he unclipped his other boot. Carried his board under an arm toward the top of the run.

"You going to make it Ajax?" Sage asked, trudging along with her board in hand as well.

The sound of snow crunching beneath their boots gave a distinctive sound in the late morning air. Overhead, the sky was the color of milk.

A solid wall of clouds threatened to unleash more snow at any moment.

"Go to Hell, all of you," Ajax said, his voice muffled. Given the number of layers enveloping his body, it was a wonder that any sound was audible at all.

How he was able to ski was anybody's guess.

Beside him, Kade reached out a hand and punched Ajax in the arm. "I bet you wish *you* were in Hell right now. Bet it's at least a little warmer than this, don't you?"

More indecipherable grumbling was the only response.

The Zoo Crew.

The self-awarded nickname for the quartet comprised of the biggest outliers in the Missoula community.

The group had formed seven years before, an outgrowth of a potent mixture of necessity and boredom. At the time, it was just the three males.

Drake and Ajax, a random pairing brought together by the University of Montana housing lottery.

Drake and Kade, a random pairing brought together by the University of Montana football team.

It took less than a month for the three to develop a kinship. All of them were just a degree or two off from the traditional western Montana homogeneity.

Each let it bother him for about 10 seconds before they came together. Reveled in it every moment since.

The basis for the Crew itself began in the spring of their freshmen year.

Less than two weeks before finals, they formed the idea to meet at least three mornings a week. Come together and get outside.

Didn't matter time of year. Didn't even matter the activity.

Strap it up and get after it. Leave the stress of the world behind for a while.

Summer was set aside for fishing. In the winter, they skied. The time in between - hiking, golfing, snowshoeing.

The specific activity wasn't important. The details would figure themselves out.

Drake reached the flag marking the top of the run first. Dropped his board to the ground. Clipped his boots into their harnesses. Strapped them down tight.

Beside him, Sage did the same, the combined sound of their clips ringing out over the steady drone of the ski lift.

A moment later, Kade wedged his boots down onto his skis. Ajax got his board ready to go.

"Alright, so what are we going for today?" Sage asked. Stood up and brushed long dark hair back from her face. Smashed a fleece cap down on it. Positioned her orange-tinted goggles down over her eyes.

"Losers buy breakfast?" Drake asked. Pulled a pair of mirrored Oakley's into place.

"Naw, we always do that," Kade countered, standing up, gripping his poles in either hand. "Besides, I'm the only one here on skis. You guys should let me win out of principal."

"And what principal would that be?" Drake asked.

"That skiing is 10 times harder than snowboarding," Kade said. "You guys owe me breakfast for being the only one here man enough to do it."

"The only reason you're *man enough to do it* is because you don't have the balls to get on a board," Ajax countered. Slid into position alongside Drake and Sage.

"I don't think that's the problem," Drake said. "There are plenty of women in town that will vouch he has balls."

"Yeah, it's his discretion that's a little bit lacking," Sage added. Mixture of disapproval and disbelief in her voice.

They all knew she was rolling her eyes behind the goggles, even if they couldn't see it.

"You've made your point," Kade said. Voice flat. Exasperated. "Same bet as usual. First pair to cross the line gets breakfast courtesy of the losers. Deal?"

"Deal," Drake said, "but no ordering wine this time, huh?"

A mischievous smile crossed Kade's face. Remained affixed as he positioned his goggles.

"I can't promise anything. It is Christmas, after all."

Without a word he disappeared down the run, his long, dark hair blowing behind him.

The rest of the Crew departed right on his heels, a plume of snow rising in their wake.

CHAPTER FOUR

Snow Plaza.

The flagship ski lodge in Western Montana. The reason people flocked in droves to Missoula every winter.

One of the many reasons most of them never left.

The front doors to an oversized A-frame lodge opened wide as the Crew ascended the stairs, beckoning them in. A confluence of light and warmth hit as they passed through, leaving the cold morning behind.

Just three days before Christmas, the crowd was much thinner than usual. The student body at the U had left the weekend before. A fair number of the regulars had already departed for their holiday sojourns.

Not quite first-day-of-the-season thin, but not far behind.

Drake and Sage were the first two inside, broad grins plastered across their faces. Behind them trudged Kade and Ajax, begrudging half-smiles in place.

"I tell you, I am famished," Sage said, eyes shining. "I feel like I could eat a cow."

"I don't know if I can eat a cow, but I have every intention of trying," Drake added, drawing a chuckle from Sage.

Behind them, Ajax and Kade both shook their heads. Ajax mumbled something unintelligible while Kade settled for, "Yeah, yeah, yeah."

The lodge in front of them was comprised of one expansive room. Round tables dotted the floor while padded benches lined the walls.

Most days every available seat was taken.

Today, it was less than one-in-three.

A stone fireplace dominated the rear of the space, grey rock mined from the Clark Fork River rolling through town. In it was a fire that was lit sometime in October, left blazing until early April.

It was the only source of heat for the entire lodge, a job it more than fulfilled.

Paired up two and two, the Crew made their way through the center of the lodge. A handful of wait staff crossed back and forth in front of them as they went. Many nodded in recognition.

Off to the left, an older couple raised a pair of coffee cups in salute. Lewis and Cynthia Hill. Long-time Snow Plaza fixtures, even longer Missoula residents.

"Who won?" Cynthia called as they passed, her wrinkled visage split into a smile.

"Score one for the good guys," Drake replied, hands spread wide.

More grumbling from Ajax and Kade behind him.

Less than 10 minutes after finishing their run, the group found their usual table in the corner. Ajax went for his customary spot closest to the fire, still bundled in his outdoor attire.

How he was able to sit that close to the flames without melting was anybody's guess.

Ajax - birth name Adam Jackson - was the first person Drake met in Missoula that wasn't in some way connected to Griz football. A trust fund kid from Boston, he had come to Missoula to be as far from the trappings of his affluent New England family as possible.

Despite the enormous financial backing at his fingertips, he had never touched a cent.

Not that he ever needed to.

Designing video games had made him one of the richest people in Montana by the time he was 22-years-old.

Three years later, he still lived in the same house off campus that he and Drake rented beginning in their sophomore year. The only differences were now they owned it, and Drake's English bulldog shared it with them.

If measured, Ajax would come in four inches above 6' tall, though it was hard for anybody to actually tell. Half the year, a tangle of loose dreadlocks hung from his head, giving him an extra boost.

The other half - like now - he was mummified in winter gear.

Not only did it mask his true height, but made it look like he weighed significantly north of his actual 150 pounds.

Sliding into a seat across from Ajax was Kade Keuhl, the first person Drake met in Montana, period.

The product of a German father and Native American mother, bits of both could be seen in his features.

Thick, dark hair that hung past his shoulders. Sharp cheekbones. Light skin. Blue eyes.

Hailing from the Flathead Reservation 60 miles north of Missoula, Kade grew up too light for the Native American community, too dark for the Caucasian contingent. Over time, he developed a raw tenacity and thick skin that made him a great athlete.

Loyal friend.

Standing a few inches under 6' tall, he carried the same sinewy physique he had when his playing days ended three years prior.

As a fire jumper that spent half of the calendar year chasing blazes all over the west, being in shape was a necessary evil.

"Alright, so what's it going to be?" Sage Keuhl asked, sliding herself into a chair beside Kade. She pulled her hat and gloves off and piled them on the table, a satisfied smile on her face.

Two years younger than the other three, Sage was the newest member of the Crew.

Growing up in the same predicament as her brother, she spent her formative years counting seconds until she could get off the rez. Once her time was served, she shot past Missoula to Bozeman for nursing school.

After completion, she returned to Missoula as an RN at St. Michael's Hospital.

When she arrived three years before, Kade invited her along on the morning outings hoping to help her connect with the community.

What he actually accomplished was to make her an indispensable part of the Crew.

"Just remember, you guys said before taking off that there would be no wine list," Ajax said. "No steak and eggs. No Crème Brule."

"I remember saying nothing about steak and eggs," Drake said, sliding out the last of the chairs and settling himself into it.

On outward appearance alone, he was the most common of the bunch. If such a word could be used to describe anybody at the table.

Blonde hair kept short, uniform in length. Blue eyes.

A build that suggested wide receiver. Maybe quarterback.

He'd been brought to Missoula from West Tennessee seven years earlier to play middle linebacker. Now that his playing days were over, there wasn't the need to remain quite so large.

At first glance, many would not take Drake for an outlier.

That illusion was shattered the moment he opened his mouth.

There are places in American where having a southern drawl isn't enough to label a person as an outlier.

Missoula is not one of those places.

"Or Crème Brule," Sage added.

"Yeah, I'm going to head this off before it goes any further," Kade said, raising a hand in the air. He waved it about until catching the attention of the waitress walking by and pointed down at the table. "The usual."

The waitress, a middle-aged redhead named Helen, nodded in reply. She'd been waiting on the Zoo Crew for three years and counting. She knew what the usual meant.

Bacon and eggs for Ajax and Kade.

Denver omelets for Drake and Sage.

"The usual, huh?" Drake said, leveling a faux serious look on his friend. "That's not much of a victory meal."

"Wasn't much of a victory," Kade said. "You beat the abominable snowman over there and a guy on skis."

"Don't give me that," Sage countered. "You even had a head start."

For the first time since leaving the house that morning, Ajax removed the scarf from around his face. Smooth caramel skin peeked out from the wall of North Face gear.

"Hey now, can't we all get along? It is Christmas, you know."

"I'll be damned, it talks," Drake said, his face flat as he stared at Ajax.

"Go to Hell," Ajax deadpanned, the table breaking into laughter.

"Hey! It *is* Christmas, you know," Drake echoed.

The table laughed harder, the two friends shaking their heads at one another.

"Speaking of which," Sage said, "what's the agenda?"

"I'm heading home this afternoon," Kade said. "Told Ma I'd cut the tree and get it set up."

"I'm here until tomorrow morning," Sage said. "Supposed to snow tonight, so I'll sack out after work and drive up first thing."

"Good call," Kade said. Shifted his attention to Ajax and Drake. "Your plans?"

Ajax's face clouded a bit. He aimed his gaze at the table, shook his head.

"I fly out Sunday morning."

Three surprised looks stared back at him. Nobody said a word.

He raised his eyes, saw their stares. Shook his head again.

"Family won't let me get away with skipping another holiday."

There was no further explanation. There didn't have to be.

"What time you fly out?" Drake asked.

"7:00."

Drake turned to Kade. "I'll be there between 8:00 and 9:00."

Ajax opened his mouth to protest. Closed it just as fast.

There was no need to argue. That's not how things were done with the Crew. He needed a ride to the airport. Christmas Eve or not, they weren't about to let him call a cab.

Before any further discussion could be had, Helen arrived, their meals in hand. She unloaded each of them in front of their corresponding person, not bothering to ask who ordered what.

Nobody had in fact ordered anything.

She set the plates down and stood back. Pressed her hands on her hips. Sighed.

"Well now, will you folks be needing anything else?"

"No, I think we're all set," Drake said.

"This is great, thanks," Sage added.

Helen nodded, took a glance around. Nobody in the lodge seemed to be in need, so she took a step forward.

"Hey, what did you guys think of that mess in Hamilton last night?"

All four exchanged blank looks.

"What happened in Hamilton last night?" Kade asked.

A conspiratorial smile spread across Helen's features. The unbridled joy of being the first to share a fresh bit of information. "You guys haven't heard? It's been all over the news."

"We've been here all morning," Drake said. "What happened?"

"I guess some guy showed up at the Ag Commission meeting and shot up the place. Just walked in with a rifle and started firing."

"Oh my God, that's awful," Sage said.

"Was anybody hurt?" Drake asked.

"That's the darnedest part of it," Helen said. Shook her head. "Just the guy himself."

"He shot himself?" Ajax asked, confusion on his face.

"No," Helen replied. "Somebody in the audience had a concealed carry and shot him. The shooter didn't hit a darn thing."

All four people around the table leaned back. Exchanged glances. Attempted to process what they'd been told.

At the other end of the room, a trio of new customers walked in and took seats.

Helen watched them settle into their chairs and sighed. Shook her head once more. "It never ends, I tell you. You kids holler if you need anything."

Drake and Sage both nodded in understanding.

All four sat in silence a moment. Thought about what Helen told them.

Just as fast, the moment passed.

They tore into their food with reckless abandon.

CHAPTER FIVE

Iron lung.

The slang term for a breathing machine.

Connected to a patient through a series of tubes, it pushes air into the lungs. Pauses. Pulls carbon dioxide back out.

Up and down, like a miniature accordion.

Force air in, draw it back out.

The movement had a mesmerizing effect as Sara Webb sat by the bed of her brother Lukas. Watched it rise and fall, never moving more than six inches in either direction.

The first hour she was there, she counted every single breath that was forced into Lukas' body. Made sure that the machine was doing its job. Checked to see that his chest moved as it should.

After a while, her eyes glazed over. Her mind wandered elsewhere, buffered by the up and down movement of the pump. By the rhythmic sound of breaths being pushed in and out.

Sara had gotten the call 16 hours before.

She was at home in her pajamas watching the newest *Duck Dynasty* when the Ravalli County Sheriff's Department rang. Asked if she was the sister of Lukas Webb.

Her first concern was that he had been in an accident. He was just a week back from Afghanistan and his driving was still a bit suspect.

Under the best of circumstances.

Which Montana in the winter certainly was not.

Never in her wildest dreams would she have imagined what they were calling her about. Lukas - kind, sweet, even-tempered Lukas - had walked into an Agriculture Commission meeting and opened fire.

It took her half an hour to get dressed and over to Hamilton Memorial Hospital, her movements slow and stilted. Her entire body was numb, shock taking hold.

There had to be some mistake.

She arrived to find a bevy of local law enforcement on the scene. All in uniform. Some carrying rifles.

They informed her that Lukas was in surgery at the moment. He had been shot three times.

If he survived, he would be under arrest for attempted murder.

No less than five times they asked to speak with her. Each time she refused. She was in no state to answer questions.

Wouldn't say a word even if they tried.

Only after an hour of back and forth did they relent. Inform her that they would be back at noon the next day for a full interrogation whether she wanted to or not.

Now, at four minutes before 12:00, she still had no idea what she was going to say to them.

Was even less sure what they thought they could learn from her.

A knock on the door behind her told Sara they were a few minutes early. She reached out and squeezed her brother's hand, his skin icy beneath her grip. She remained in place a moment before releasing it and rising, turning toward the door.

A man in his early 50s with thinning red hair and a prodigious midsection stood in the doorway, his hat in hand. He nodded as Sara turned to face him, his thin lips pressed tight.

"Ma'am, I'm Sheriff Jacob Pratt."

Sara already knew who he was. His face had been plastered on every post in Ravalli County the month before for election season.

Why he campaigned so hard for an uncontested race, nobody was quite sure.

"Good morning, Sheriff," Sara said, her voice even, stiff.

"If you don't mind, I'd like to ask you some questions about your brother."

Sara nodded. There was no need to say anything. She'd already agreed to answer what she knew the night before.

She followed Pratt out into the hall, past a pair of deputies flanking the door. Both eyed her as she left, equal parts curiosity and mistrust.

The Sheriff said nothing as he led her out of the post-op ward and into the main hall of the hospital. Harsh fluorescent lights gleamed off of polished floors as they walked.

Sara's shoes clicked beneath her. The Sheriff's overloaded belt groaned with strain.

The pair walked in silence until they reached the cafeteria.

"Coffee?" Pratt asked.

Sara answered with a sharp twist of the neck. Said nothing.

Opting against any for himself, he led her to the back corner of the room. Chose an isolated table and positioned himself against the wall.

Left Sara to take a seat on the opposite side.

The only possible place she could look was straight back at him.

Pratt dropped his hat crown side down on the table and slid into a seat. He waited for Sara to do the same before leaning forward onto his elbows and lowering his voice.

Glancing around the room to make sure nobody was listening.

"Sara, before we get started, I want you to know that we in no way believe you were involved in what happened last night."

Sara nodded. Remained silent.

"But do you have any idea why Lukas would do something like this?"

The familiar tug of tears pulled at the underside of Sara's eyes. She pressed them hard together and drew in a mighty sniff. Waited for the moment to pass.

When she spoke, her voice betrayed the smallest of cracks.

"I didn't even know he was gone. He went to lie down after an early dinner. I thought he was asleep, but he must have snuck out the back door."

Pratt listened without taking notes, his face screwed up in concern.

"And did he seem like anything was wrong?"

Sara's brow furrowed as she leaned back a few inches. Stared at the Sheriff like he was crazy.

"Like anything was wrong? Ten days ago, he was on patrol outside Fallujah. One night he gets a call to come home and bury his father. There hasn't been a time when something wasn't wrong in a while."

The top of Pratt's scalp was visible as he bowed his head in concession.

"I am very sorry for your loss. Mitch Webb was a good man."

There was no sound as Sara pressed her mouth closed and nodded.

She'd dealt with enough faux sympathy in the last week. She didn't need it from him, too.

"So you're telling me there was no indication? Nothing at all last night that might have tipped you off that he had hostile intentions?"

Sara blew a long, slow breath out through her nose. Made sure he heard it. Shook her head from side to side.

"Like I said, we haven't had a normal day since he got back. He's been in Afghanistan the last eight months. That's a 12-hour time difference, in the desert.

"His body clock, internal temperature, everything is off. I thought he was going to bed."

The slightest bit of frustration was creeping into her voice. She stared back at the Sheriff, meeting his gaze.

Almost dared him to challenge her on it.

Pratt seemed to sense the growing animosity within her. Opted to switch directions.

"The weapon recovered from the scene was a Winchester 30.06. Any idea where he got it?"

Sara bobbed her head. "It was dad's rifle. He kept it on the rack in the truck."

"Just like that? He kept it in the truck?"

Another nod. "He used it when he was working the cows, in case a bear or mountain lion came around."

"So your brother was familiar with the weapon?"

"We all were. Dad taught us how to shoot it."

Pratt raised his eyebrows. "That's an awful lot of firepower."

The ire continued to ebb away at Sara's resolve. "Lukas was an Army sniper. I think he can handle a 30 gauge."

A bit of color flushed Pratt's cheeks. "I meant for you."

"What does that have to do with anything?"

A tense moment passed, each side staring at the other.

For the previous 16 hours, Sara had been scared. She'd been worried that her brother might not make it. Concerned with how she could handle burying her entire family in the same week.

Now she was getting angry.

This was starting to feel less and less like an interview.

Closer to a witch hunt.

As if he could read her thoughts, Pratt leaned in close. "Miss Webb, I can appreciate how difficult this must be for you. And I assure you, I am only trying to figure this thing out."

Sara shrugged. Said nothing.

"At the same time," Pratt continued, "your brother walked into a public forum and opened fire last night."

Sara waited for him to continue.

He did not.

"Meaning?"

"Meaning that is a very serious offense."

Sara leaned back a moment and exhaled again. Swallowed down the bile rising in the back of her throat. Stared across at the Sheriff.

"So what happens when you find out why?" she asked.

"What happens?" Pratt asked. "Your brother discharged a firearm in a public place. Fired a gun designed to take down an elk at human beings. He is going to jail for a very long time.

"To be honest, I don't much care why."

Pratt stood, his cheeks flushed red. Took up his hat from the table. Stared down at her.

The words hit Sara square in the stomach. Forced the wind from her lungs.

She sat with her jaw slack, unable to respond.

"You should both be considered lucky that he didn't hit anybody," Pratt said. "I don't think I need to remind you that Montana is a death penalty state."

He spun on his heel and left without another word.

CHAPTER SIX

The last of the bags was heavy.

Extremely heavy.

Drake's shoulders screamed in protest as he hefted them from the floor. Carried them down the stairs. Loaded them into the bed of his truck.

Beside it stood Ava Zargoza, the left side of her mouth curled up into a smirk.

"And here I thought you were some kind of big strong football player."

"Who said I wasn't?" Drake asked.

"Don't give me that. I heard you grunting."

"That wasn't me grunting from exertion," Drake said. "My head hurt trying to add up how much it's going to cost you to check those things."

Ava arched on eyebrow. "They're not *that* heavy."

Drake circled around the bed of his truck and slid in behind the wheel. "You are aware that airlines have a 50-pound weight limit right? That you can't wrap up a baby elephant and try to check it through?"

Opposite him, Ava climbed in and slammed the door closed. Looked up at the second story walk-up that had been her home the previous four months.

"You sure you've got everything?" Drake asked. Gazed up at the apartment as well. "Shower rod? Bed post? Kitchen sink?"

Ava was a third-year law student from the LSU School of Law. Displaced by Hurricane Wanda, she had found herself assigned to the University of Montana by virtue of her place in the alphabetical pecking order.

She was the very last person to choose.

Montana was the very last destination to be chosen.

Not once in three months had she missed an opportunity to point out either.

Ava shifted her attention from the apartment to Drake. "I've been packed and ready for three days now."

Drake coughed out a laugh. "I think you mean three months."

A smile creased Ava's features. The skin crinkled around her brown eyes, her face framed by hair hanging in dark ringlets.

The engine of the truck whined once in protest as Drake turned the key. Kicked to life as warm air burst forth through the dash.

This day had been a long time coming.

For the entire semester, Drake and Ava had been partners in the Montana Legal Services clinic. Free legal service for the poor and indigent residents in the community.

Most of the time the work was mundane, boring even.

College students contesting MIP charges. Amicable divorces. The occasional property line dispute.

Twice though, things had gotten ugly.

Very ugly.

The first had left Drake with a broken hand. Ava with a broken leg.

Only in the last month had she gotten back to walking under her own power. Even at that, her gait was marred by a limp.

On the second occasion, Drake and Ava had found themselves tied together near a creek bed 20 miles from town.

Neither one had been hurt, but they were both lucky to be alive.

And they knew it.

After the first incident, Ava vowed she would stick out the remainder of the year in Missoula.

After the second, she informed Drake she was heading back to Louisiana at the end of the semester.

He accepted the news without protest, despite a bit of sadness he never dared show her.

The afternoon traffic was light as Drake angled his truck across town. Avoided the freeway in favor of the city streets.

One last chance to show Ava what she'd be leaving. Maybe even snag a few extra minutes in the car with her.

"So do you think you'll miss us at all?" Drake asked. Kept his gaze aimed at the road.

"Us?"

Drake waved a hand at the window. "Yeah, Missoula. You think you'll miss it?"

"Oh, yeah, terribly," Ava deadpanned.

The words drew a smile from Drake.

"Come on, it's what, 65, 70, in Baton Rouge right now? Sounds miserable."

Ava pulled her heavy pea coat out a few inches. Looked down at the designer jeans she was wearing. At the sheer blouse atop a black lace camisole.

"Not having to wear a parka anymore? Miserable isn't quite the word I'd choose."

This time, she drew a laugh from Drake. A shake of the head for good measure.

"That I can't argue with. After being the most overdressed person in Montana for four months, you'll fit right in down on the Bayou."

Ava smirked. Stared out the window as a sign welcomed them to the Missoula International Airport.

"I'm taking that as a compliment."

"You should," Drake said. Swung around to the front of the terminal. "This town could use a bit more class."

The truck slid to a stop right along the front curb, not another car in sight. Drake set the flashers to blinking and climbed out, heard Ava do the same on the opposite side.

He hefted the bags from the back and carried them inside, Ava limping along beside him.

Both remained silent as she went to the counter and checked in, Drake loading the bags straight onto the conveyor. The attendant behind the counter pretended not to notice that they were both well north of 50 pounds.

Slapped a pink HEAVY sticker on them just the same.

Boarding pass in hand, Ava led Drake past the stuffed brown bear that welcomed visitors to Missoula. Past the sole gift shop. Up to the single security line with two bored TSA agents.

Everything decked out for the holidays.

Still not another person to be seen.

"Told you there was no need to be here two hours early," Drake said.

Ava smiled in concession. Shook her head.

"Yeah, yeah. I figured I'd give you one small victory before leaving."

Drake matched the smile.

Just as fast, it faded away.

"Listen, I know coming to Missoula wasn't your idea, but for what it's worth, I'm glad you did."

A wistful expression crossed Ava's face.

"You know, I might have liked it a little bit more here than I let on."

"Well, to be fair, nobody could have hated it as much as you pretended to."

The expression changed from wistful to a smile. Ava extended her arms and slid them around Drake. Pulled him tight.

"I will miss you," she said. "You might be the only thing I can say that about, though."

Drake smiled against the side of her head.

"Just remember, you're always welcome to come back. If I end up deciding to hang a shingle after graduation, I could use a partner."

"I'll remember that," Ava said. Squeezed tighter. Released and pulled back, her hands on his ribs.

The two stared at each other another moment.

Ava pushed back in for one more hug. Kissed him on the cheek.

"Thank you for saving my life," she whispered. "Twice."

This time, Drake squeezed her tighter. "You're welcome. Merry Christmas."

"Merry Christmas," Ava replied.

The two released and took a step back. Exchanged a nod.

Drake watched as Ava told the agents she still had metal rods in her leg. Stood rigid while they passed wands over her body. Grabbed her bag and trudged up the stairs toward the gate.

At the top, she turned and waved one last time.

Drake returned the gesture.

They remained that way a full moment. Ava was the first to break away, disappearing around the corner.

Drake waited just long enough to ensure she wasn't coming back and spun on a heel. Exited through the front door.

Went back to his truck still parked on the curb.

CHAPTER SEVEN

For the first time in two days, Sara slept.

Not the deep, easy sleep of someone home in their own bed. The fitful, restless sleep of someone slumped in a hospital room chair.

Someone wracked with worry for the person in the bed beside them.

One moment, Sara was alert. Her gaze was aimed at the iron lung moving up and down. The hospital was semi-active.

The next, her chin was on her chest. The lights were dim.

The breathing apparatus was the only sound.

Sara blinked herself awake. Sort of. Raised her head and rubbed the side of it.

Let out a groan.

"You should go home for the night. Get some rest," a voice said through the semi-darkness.

At the sound of it, Sara's heartrate spiked. Her eyes popped open wide. Her breath caught in her chest.

On the far side of the bed sat a solitary figure. His body was silhouetted against the opposite wall, but she knew the voice well enough to know who it was without a full visual.

"Rink," she whispered.

The silhouette nodded. "Sorry I wasn't here sooner. We played in Cody last night. Spent most of the day on a bus counting minutes."

Sara nodded. "Thank you for coming. You're the first person that has."

Rink let the statement pass without comment. "Is it true?"

"Depends. What have you heard?"

Rink shifted his attention down to Lukas. Took in the breathing tube affixed over his mouth. The myriad of IV's hooked to his arm.

"Just what they said on the news. Lukas walked into a commissioner's meeting last night and started firing. Some guy in the crowd was packing, shot him down."

Sara nodded. "That's about all I know, too. I wasn't there when it happened."

Rink shifted his attention back to her. "The cops didn't tell you?"

A derisive snort rolled out of Sara. More reaction than response. It slid from her before she even realized she was doing it.

"All they've told me so far is the minute he wakes up, he's going to jail."

Rink winced. Drew in a breath between his teeth.

"When do they expect that will be?"

"One of the bullets punctured his lung. Right now they're keeping him in a coma until he's strong enough to breathe on his own."

Rink sat in the darkened room, his features clouded. He looked at his friend lying in the bed. Heard the breathing tube, the heartrate monitor calling out a steady cadence.

"There any way he didn't do it?"

A dozen thoughts went through Sara's head. She pushed them back one at a time. "No."

Rink nodded. "What can I do to help?"

Sara shook her head. A slow, exhausted movement. "Right now? Nothing."

"And later?"

Her mouth opened and closed several times. Tried to find the words. "When he comes around, he's going to be in a world of trouble."

The statement hung in the air for several long minutes.

Weighed on Sara. Wormed its way into Rink.

He turned his head and faced her. "I might be able to help on that front."

"You might be able to help?"

Rink nodded again. "I know a guy. Let me make a call."

"Is this guy a lawyer?"

Rink's right eye narrowed. He gave a non-committal twist of the head. "Yes."

"You know I can't pay much, especially after the funeral and everything."

"That won't matter. You say the word and I'll call him tonight."

Sara stared at Rink for a moment before shifting her gaze to Lukas.

"Do it. I'm not going to lose him, too."

CHAPTER EIGHT

Snoring.

Very loud, interminable snoring.

It was the cadence that accompanied Drake the entire drive to Hamilton. One long inhalation of air that resembled a choking hyena.

A pause.

A slow, elongated release.

Between every third or fourth round, a slight puff of gas. The feeling of nausea sweeping in right behind it.

The source of this audio and olfactory crescendo was an English bulldog curled up on the front seat beside him. Short and compact, her entire body was wedged tight against the seat back.

Drake had tried to sneak out of the house that morning without her, but Suzy Q would not allow it. Whined until he relented. Bounded up into the truck with practiced movements.

Curling up, she was fast asleep before they reached the Missoula city limits.

Drake stared out as he drove south through the Bitterroot Valley. The morning was cold and clear, just another in the four-month winter stretch in western Montana known as The Greys.

One carbon copy of a day after another.

He kept the radio off. The only sounds were Suzy Q on the seat beside him and the steady blast of the heater.

Saturday morning traffic was non-existent as he pushed on, the 30-mile drive taking less than an hour. The entire time, his mind worked through what he might find waiting for him.

The only thing Rink had said the night before was he needed help. Not him personally, but a friend.

Drake told him he'd been down in the morning without hesitation.

No further details were given.

There was no reason for Drake to believe that it had anything to do with the shooting a few nights before. For whatever reason though, he couldn't shake the notion.

Knowing Rink, it could be anything from a car accident to a bar fight gone bad.

The only thing Drake knew for sure was Rink had said it was urgent and that he needed to meet with him in particular.

For Rink - a satellite member of the Crew himself - to exclude the others could only mean one thing.

He needed a lawyer.

Drake slid his truck to a stop in front of the Hamilton Memorial Hospital and turned it off. Rink's rig was parked a few spots over, but there was no sign of him.

Drake pulled a woven blanket over Q and left her sleeping on the front seat. She cracked an eye in response as he did so, but made no effort to follow.

The front doors parted to the side as he approached, a plastic placard pointing him toward the cafeteria.

Over the last few years, he'd spent a fair bit of time in St. Michael's Hospital visiting Sage. He knew the basic floor plan without ever having stepped foot in Hamilton Memorial.

Cafeteria to the left. Emergency Room toward the right. Surgery ward somewhere in the back. Myriad of departments and clinics filling in the gaps.

Efficient, if not imaginative.

Drake stepped into the cafeteria at three minutes before 10:00 to find it less than half empty. A couple of heads turned his way as he entered, sizing him up.

Dressed in jeans and a knit sweater, he was dismissed just as fast. Another concerned family member, nothing more.

In the corner of the room, a hand went into the air. With dark red curls shaped into a widow's peak and a thick scar running right at his hairline, there was no mistaking the owner.

Rink.

Drake raised his chin in recognition and cut a path through the tables toward the back. Rink rose from his seat as he approached, thrusting a hand out in front of him.

"Thanks for coming," Rink said as way of a greeting.

It was far and away the most formal thing Drake had ever heard him say.

This couldn't be good.

"Absolutely," Drake said, returning the shake. "I just hope I'm able to help."

Rink nodded and released the shake. Extended the same hand toward a young woman with dishwater blonde hair across from him. "Drake, this is Sara Webb."

Drake extended a hand toward her. Took in the puffiness around her eyes, the red-rimmed nostrils. Noticed that while she was slender and appeared to be of medium height, there was no way of knowing either for sure.

An oversized cardigan was wrapped around her, seeming to swallow her whole.

"Pleasure to meet you," Drake said, her hand cold within his. He grabbed a chair from an adjacent table and pulled it up on the end. Sat facing forward, Rink and Sara on either side.

A dozen thoughts ran through his head as he did so. He could tell by the girl's expression, by Rink's stilted approach, that this was serious.

Decided to let them take the lead.

A moment later, Rink did so.

"I don't know how much you've been keeping up with the news the last few days," he began.

Drake felt the feeling from before kick up in the back of his mind. Kept his face neutral.

"But I'm guessing by now you've heard about the shooting that took place night before last?"

Pieces clicked into place in Drake's mind. He leaned his head back an inch or two, twisted his gaze to Sara.

"Webb."

She nodded. "My brother."

"And I'm guessing since you asked me to meet you at Memorial..." Drake said. Let his voice trail off, the implication clear.

"Yes," she said. "He's here."

Drake flicked his gaze over to Rink, back to Sara. "How's he doing?"

She swallowed hard, lines forming on either side of her mouth. If she'd slept at all the last two days, it hadn't been much. "He's in a coma right now."

That was true to the story he'd read in *The Missoulian* that morning.

Still, he'd had to ask.

"I'm very sorry."

Sara pressed her lips together as if to mumble a thank you. No sound came out though.

Silence fell over the table.

Not easy, amicable silence.

Heavy, awkward silence.

Drake turned his attention away from the table. Looked at a family eating nearby. A harried mother trying in vain to corral two young children, a third with food smeared all over her face.

The corner of his mouth turned up in a smile.

He was stalling and he knew it.

"Forgive me if I sound harsh when asking this, because I don't mean to," he said. "What is it you were hoping for me to do?"

The news reports stated that Lukas Webb had been shot at the scene. If he was now in a coma, that meant his injuries were far more severe than they had let on.

Drake had never been a fan of doing estate work, but if drafting a will was what Rink had called him in to do, he would.

Without question.

There was a pause as Sara and Rink stared across at each other. The silence between them lasted long enough that Drake gazed at each one in turn, his brow furrowed.

After what seemed an eternity, Sara nodded.

Rink leaned in close. Lowered his voice. Cast a gaze about to make sure nobody was listening.

"Right now they're keeping Lukas in a coma for his own safety," Rink began.

As he spoke, Sara's eyes slid closed.

"One of the bullets pierced his lung. They're keeping him sedated and on a breathing machine until he is strong enough to be taken off."

Drake nodded, pretending to follow.

This complicated things tremendously. If they weren't looking for a will to be drafted, there wasn't a lot else he could assist with.

"Standing watch outside his door right now is a pair of armed deputies," Rink said. "The second he comes to, they intend to arrest him, send him over to Deer Lodge."

Drake nodded again. A few lines in his mind connected what he was hearing. Still, there were a lot of gaps.

"And so?" he prompted.

"There's no doubt my brother walked into that meeting and fired those shots," Sara said.

Drake shifted his gaze to her. Was almost taken aback by the intensity of her stare on him.

"But if he did it, he damned sure had a good reason."

"Okay," Drake said.

Once more, Sara and Rink exchanged a glance.

"I want you to find out what it was."

CHAPTER NINE

Drake's jaw dropped.

Not in an attempt to make a point.

A completely unrehearsed, natural reaction.

His eyes bulged and his mouth hung open as he stared at Sara.

"Look, I truly am sorry for the predicament you're in. I am. But I'm a law student, I don't think this sort of thing is in my job description."

Sara fell silent. Looked down at her hands twisted together in her lap.

Drake watched her a moment before rotating his head at the neck to look at Rink.

Rink met his eye. Motioned toward the service area with the top of his head.

"Buy you a cup of coffee?"

Anybody that had met Drake knew he didn't drink coffee. It was a thinly-veiled attempt to get him alone for a moment.

Drake knew it. Nodded his ascent.

"Excuse us," Rink said, rising from his chair.

Across from him Sara sat in silence, her attention still aimed down at her hands.

Drake rose and followed Rink. They waited until they were almost to the door of the serving line. Turned to make sure Sara wasn't paying them any mind.

Ducked around the corner.

"They need somebody that can keep Lukas out of jail," Rink said.

No preamble. No lead-in. Straight to the point.

"No, what they need is a private investigator," Drake said.

"Since when has that made any difference to you?"

Drake opened his mouth to respond. Closed it just as fast.

Rink wasn't wrong, and they both knew it.

"Still," he said, "I almost got my partner killed twice doing that sort of thing. That's the reason she got on a plane back to Louisiana yesterday."

Rink's face betrayed surprise. "What? Ava's gone?"

"Ava's gone," Drake said. Nodded for emphasis.

"Damn," Rink said. Stared off into space a moment. Allowed his face to twist into a half-smile. "And I never got a chance to take her out."

"Exactly," Drake said. "That's not what being a lawyer is about. I can't keep poking bee hives, getting my friends in trouble, over this stuff."

Rink stared right at him. Bore his gaze into Drake. "You know if you need anything, *anything*, on this one, I have your back."

"I know that," Drake said. "And I know I owe you-"

He was cut off by a wave. "Bullshit. We don't keep score and you know it."

Drake shoved his hands into the pockets of his jeans. Exhaled through his nose. Stared at Rink a moment.

Shifted his gaze past him to Sara sitting in the corner.

"Are you kidding me?" Drake asked. Made no effort to hide the annoyance in his voice.

"What?" Rink asked. Turned to see what Drake was staring at.

"Stay here."

Drake left Rink standing in the corner. Walked back through the dining room. Came to a stop behind his chair on the end of the table.

On one side sat Sara, her hands still folded in her lap.

On the other sat a woman with white-grey hair cut short. Wire-rimmed glasses. A leather jacket and blouse with jeans.

Drake recognized her the moment he saw her sit down.

The woman turned and smiled as Drake approached. Extended a bony hand toward him. "Good morning, Paula Goslin."

"Good morning," Drake replied. Tried to keep his voice curt, but not hostile.

Didn't do a very good job at it. "Drake Bell."

"Nice to meet you," Goslin said. "And how do you know Ms. Webb here?"

"I'm her attorney," Drake said. Spat the words out. Wanted the woman to know he knew what she was up to and he wasn't going to stand for it.

The smile fled from her features.

The skin around her eyes tightened as she stared at Drake. Reached for a purse on the chair beside her. Rose to go.

"Well, it was very nice meeting you, Sara. I do hope we can speak again sometime."

The tone of her voice did not match the expression on her face. She stared daggers at Drake as she departed, pure venom in her eyes.

Drake matched her with every bit of vitriol he could muster.

As she left, Drake felt Rink step up behind him.

"Who was that?" Rink asked.

Drake ignored the question. Shifted his focus to Sara. "Have they said yet when they expect to wake your brother?"

Sara's mouth dropped open a half-inch. She stared at Drake a moment before closing it, her mind grasping his question.

"Um, a doctor this morning said probably a week. Allow his body recover a full seven days before attempting to let it fend for itself."

Drake nodded. "That's good. As long as he's sedated, we know where he is. They can't try to arrest him or move him anywhere."

"Dude, who *was* that?" Rink repeated.

"Paula Goslin," Drake said. Turned his attention back to the door. Looked to make sure she was gone. "Ravalli County Attorney."

He blinked. Shifted his focus down to Sara. "The woman that will be trying to prosecute your brother the minute he wakes up."

A look of shock passed over Sara's features. "I knew she looked familiar," she whispered.

"Does that mean you'll look into it?" Rink asked.

Drake stared out through the windows above Sara. Watched as Goslin walked across the parking lot. Climbed into a Silverado truck with all the bells and whistles, at least three sizes too big for her.

Leather jacket and oversized pickup.

Telltale signs of a wannabe rancher.

"I'll see what I can do."

CHAPTER TEN

Saturday afternoon.

Every single week, Holt Tierney met with his ranch supervisor. Didn't matter what time of year, whether it was Christmas or his wife's birthday.

Saturday was the end of the work week. Tierney met with his supervisor.

Sometimes it took less than half an hour. Others, it could go for two or more.

Either way, they sat down in Tierney's office and hashed things out until they were done.

On this particular Saturday, Tierney's mind was a hundred different places.

Christmas coming in two days. The expected snowfall just a few hours off. The next round of vaccinations for his herd.

The shooting the night before last.

The second meeting on his afternoon agenda.

Tierney sat with his polished Ropers propped on the corner of his desk. Ever the gentlemen rancher, he was dressed in starched Wrangler's. Green and brown plaid pearl-snap shirt. Buckskin colored blazer.

A snow white Stetson sat upside down beside him.

A plain manila folder was open on his lap. In it were the usual print-outs his supervisor had prepared. His eyes danced over the numbers as his right hand tugged at a bushy grey mustache.

"As you can see, things are still plugging along," Rex Johnson said. The words were said with a bit of finality that raised Tierney's gaze from the pages.

He'd barely heard a word Johnson said.

Still, he knew enough to know when it was his turn to speak.

"Mhmm," Tierney said. Studied the man across from him, supervisor of his ranch the last 12 years. Employee for a dozen more before that.

Johnson was an affable man. He was thick throughout, a quality that extended even to his lips and hands. His cheeks were always rosy tinted and a thick shock of light brown hair was fast approaching white.

For whatever reason, Tierney had always liked him.

The enormity of that fact, given that Tierney very rarely liked anybody, was not lost on either of them.

"Yes, everything looks good," Tierney said. Closed the folder and tossed it down on the desk. Made a show of sighing and rubbing his thumb and forefinger over his eyes. "You'll have to forgive me, it's been a long couple of days."

"No apology necessary," Johnson said. Waved an enormous paw for emphasis. "That would have shook up anybody."

"Hmm," Tierney said. Felt blood flush behind his cheeks. "Big plans for the holiday?"

The statement was a blatant attempt to change the subject. They both knew it, but pretended not to.

"Just the usual. The kids are driving down from Missoula. Mary Beth's cooking dinner. Thank you very much for the generous bonus, by the way, sir."

This time it was Tierney's turn to wave a hand. "No thanks needed, Rex. You earned it."

Hat in hand, Johnson rose. Offered a downward nod so intense it bent him over at the waist.

"You have a Merry Christmas, sir. I'll see you back here on Wednesday."

"You too," Tierney said. The words sounded hollow, even in his own ears. "Please give my best to the family."

"Will do," Johnson promised. Retreated from the room without another word.

He was gone no more than a minute when a knock sounded at the door.

Tierney returned the thumb and forefinger to his eyes and pressed them down hard. He kept them there until bright lights started to pop behind his eyelids.

"Come in, Hank."

The door slid open a few inches as the second appointment of the afternoon entered.

These meetings had started two months prior. They followed right on the heels of the meeting with Johnson, though the two couldn't have been more different.

As far as Tierney could tell, Johnson had no idea who McIlvaine was or what he was doing there.

There was no reason to give the answer to either question.

Tierney pulled the hand away from his eyes. Blinked several times in succession. Waited as they adjusted back to the late afternoon light. Turned his attention to the visitor.

Hank McIlvaine walked across the room and dropped himself into the chair Johnson was just using without a sound. After the oversized appearance of the man before him, his wiry build was a harsh juxtaposition.

Everything about him stood in stark contrast to Johnson. Dark hair and beard shorn all the same length. Grey eyes. Skin that never tanned. A frame that didn't deviate from 165 pounds.

In two months, Tierney had yet to see him smile.

The air was heavy between them for the better part of two minutes before either side said a word, both surveying the other.

Tierney anxious, his blue eyes probing for any indication of an opening.

McIlvaine bored, his face indiscernible.

"Anything new to report?" Tierney asked. His voice was a bit higher than necessary, his brow pinched a little tighter.

"He's in a coma," McIlvaine said. "They intend to keep him there for the week."

"He's *alive?*" Tierney asked. Shook his head in disbelief.

McIlvaine raised his eyebrows. Rolled his eyes beneath them. "Guy's a week out of Special Forces. Pretty tough sumbitch."

"Still, how many rounds did he take?"

"Three."

Tierney's brow pinched a bit tighter. "Three? That's it? How many did you fire?"

"More than three," McIlvaine said.

He made no attempt to elaborate.

Tierney didn't push it.

"Channel 3 called today and asked to do a brief interview tonight," McIlvaine said.

"What did you tell them?"

"Told them I had to check my calendar. That, of course, being you."

"Mmm," Tierney said. Nodded. Tried to hide his pleasure at being consulted before any decisions were made. "You alone?"

"Me and some lady named Goslin."

Tierney nodded again. "Do it. Paula will cover most of the talking. Just look at the camera and try to appear sorry. Be humble."

"Anything else?"

The comment wasn't quite a sneer. Wasn't far off either.

Tierney decided to let it pass.

"I'll be here with my family the next couple of days. Feel free to take off. Be back first thing Tuesday morning."

"Nowhere to go," McIlvaine said. "I'll be around if you need anything. Keep an eye on Webb at the hospital."

A grunt of agreement was all Tierney offered. "Also, my annual Winter Ball is next weekend. You'll of course be on hand."

"Guest or employee?"

"Yes," Tierney replied.

McIlvaine nodded in understanding. Rose to go without further comment.

Tierney opened his mouth to add something more. Decided against it.

Watched the man leave without a sound.

CHAPTER ELEVEN

Blood.

Lots and lots of blood.

Drake watched with a bemused expression as it splashed across the television screen. Sprayed in various directions. Dripped from every possible surface.

"Remind me what the point in this one is again?"

Across the room, Ajax stood front and center. He held a video game controller in his hand. Stood on the balls of his feet, body coiled for action.

"These guys were looking for something to rival *Call of Duty*," he said, panting. "Came up with a zombie apocalypse spin on it."

The expression remained on Drake's face. "I see."

"Hey, don't go judging me," Ajax said. "I don't create the concepts, I just design the damn things."

A smile cracked Drake's face. He watched as Ajax held the controller in front of him like a broadsword. Swung it in vicious swipes through the air.

With each one, the tangle of dreadlocks atop his head flipped into a different arrangement.

A new spray of bloody pulp appeared on screen.

"You sure you don't want in on this?" Ajax asked.

Drake cocked an eyebrow. Looked down at Suzy Q stretched out beside him, her head on his thigh.

"I'm good, but thanks. Sage should be here any second now anyway."

"Suit yourself," Ajax said. Resumed his stance. Swung his imaginary weapon in a wide half-arc. Removed an undead's head from its shoulders.

Sprayed blood across the entirety of their LCD television.

Another smirk slid out of Drake as he watched. Shook his head as he smelled Sage's arrival long before he heard it.

With a pat to Q's shoulder, he rose from his seat and turned to see Sage walking down the hall toward them, a pair of enormous pizzas from The Firetower in her hands.

"You guys think you've got that thing loud enough?" she asked in lieu of hello. "Could hear it clear out on the driveway."

Drake pointed at Ajax. "You know how he gets when he's working."

"I think the whole neighborhood knows," Sage replied.

Ajax finished the level he was playing, oblivious to them both. When the last monster fell before his blade, he flipped the control into a chair.

Turned and wiped a hand across the sheen on his forehead. Went straight for the kitchen.

"For the record, I heard you both the entire time. I'm just choosing to ignore it."

Sage carried the pizzas around to the front of the couch. Spread them out side by side on the coffee table.

"Funny how The Firetower has a way of doing that."

"Noble even, isn't it?" Drake added. Resumed his spot. Shooed Q onto the floor. Wiped her hair from the seat beside him.

Ajax returned from the kitchen and extended a bottle of water toward each of them.

Nobody bothered with plates.

Three bites in, Drake lowered his slice. Used the remote to shift the TV from gaming gore to local programming. Flipped through the channels.

Stopped on the fourth one he came to.

Gone was any interest in his pizza.

He didn't notice Q staring in longing at the slice beside him. Didn't pick up on Sage and Ajax casting glances his way.

Instead, he focused his attention at Paula Goslin on the screen. A man with hair and beard all shorn the same length stood beside her.

A graphic across the bottom of the screen read: **State To Pursue Maximum Penalty For Commission Shooting.**

He turned the volume up several notches, almost matching what Ajax was playing at a few moments before.

Nobody in the room said anything as he leaned forward. Rested his elbows on his knees.

"We have worked very hard to make Hamilton the type of community people can be proud of," Goslin said. Stared in earnest at the camera. "There is just no place for this sort of public destruction in our town."

A young reporter with teased out blonde hair and a silk blouse pulled the microphone back. "I understand that the shooter was taking part in the meeting, then chose to step outside halfway through?"

Goslin nodded. "Yes, and for whatever reason, he decided to open fire on a lawful and peaceful public assembly."

The microphone was again pulled back. "Now, Mr. McIlvaine, it has been reported that you were the one that managed to put the shooter down before he did any real damage?"

The man nodded. Glanced into the camera. Looked away just as fast.

"Yes, ma'am. I've had a concealed carry permit since leaving the military. It's the kind of thing you pray you never have to use, but you're glad you have when you do."

The blonde nodded. Pulled back the microphone. "I think I speak for the people of Hamilton when I say they're glad you had it, too."

She thrust the microphone back to him. Unsure what to say, he stared at it, up at her. A shy smile crossed his face. "I guess so, ma'am."

"And Ms. Goslin, word is the state will pursue the highest possible penalty allowable in this kind of case?"

"Yes, that is correct," Goslin said. "This sort of action goes well beyond the usual disorderly conduct charges of discharging a weapon in a public place.

"This was nothing short of premeditated, attempted murder. Lukas Webb will go to prison for the rest of his life for this."

Drake's jaw clenched. He remained silent.

Onscreen, the blonde pulled the microphone back one last time. Turned to face the camera.

"Direct from the mouth of Ravalli County Attorney Paula Goslin, the state will be seeking life imprisonment for the shooting that took place two nights ago.

"Reporting live from Hamilton, Montana, I'm Susan Smarte, KGRZ News."

Drake sat immobile for a moment. Reached out with the remote. Lowered the volume. Leaned back against the couch.

The three bites of pizza churned in his stomach. He worked his tongue around inside his mouth, trying to find some saliva.

"You alright?" Sage asked.

Drake nodded. A stiff, slow movement. "Yeah. Things just got a lot more interesting, that's all."

Sage's mouth formed into a circle. She stared at Drake a moment. Shifted her attention to Ajax.

"You remember the thing about Rink and his friend?" Ajax said.

"Yeah?" Sage asked.

Ajax motioned with his chin toward the television. "It just got a lot more interesting."

Her mouth fell all the way open. This time she started on Ajax, shifted her attention over to Drake.

"What does this mean?"

Drake ran a hand back over his hair. Pursed his lips in thought.

"There's no denying he did it. Regardless what his reasoning was, he walked into a crowded commission meeting and started firing.

"Thing is, now instead of being on the hook for a year and change - maybe less - in jail, he's up against life."

All three people leaned back. Stared off into space.

Said nothing.

CHAPTER TWELVE

Cold.

Miserable, early morning, Montana-before-the-sun-rises cold.

It first greeted Drake as he stepped out of his house for the morning. Enveloped him as he walked to his truck. Penetrated to the bone as he waited for the defrost to clear his windshield.

Stayed there almost the entire way to Hamilton.

His fingers had just regained feeling when he pulled into the Hamilton Memorial Hospital parking lot. No sooner had he gotten warm than it was time to park and walk inside.

A vicious circle that anybody who has ever spent a winter in Montana knows all too well.

Drake passed through the front doors four minutes before 7:00. He hooked a hard left and headed straight for the cafeteria. Took up the same spot in the corner they'd used the day before.

Unloaded his shoulder bag and waited.

It took less than a minute.

Walking side-by-side, both resembling extras from *The Walking Dead*, entered Sara and Rink. Neither one spoke as they approached.

Both strode straight and purposeful. Kept their gaze averted. Took up chairs opposite of Drake.

Rink offered a terse nod by way of greeting. Pressed his lips tight together. Said nothing.

"Morning," Sara said. Tucked an errant strand of hair behind her ear.

"Good morning," Drake said. Pulled a legal pad and pen from his bag. "Thank you for meeting with me so early. I'm sorry I had to ask for a 7:00 start time, but I'm expected in Ronan at noon."

The faintest hint of a smile tugged at the corner of Rink's mouth. "No worries. I know better than to keep the Kuehl's waiting."

Drake smirked. "I've been told to relay you're welcome to join us."

"I know that," Rink said. "But I'm good, thanks."

Drake nodded. He had expected as much.

"I don't mind meeting this early," Sara said, pulling them back on track. "I can't sleep anyway. This gives me something else to think about."

Drake nodded again. Slid the tablet and pen in front of him. Laced his fingers atop them.

"Alright. We established yesterday that you weren't there for the actual shooting. I feel like everything we're going to get on that has already been said by the media at this point.

"So I figured we'd skip it if that's okay?"

Sara nodded in agreement.

"Besides, you mentioned wanting to find out why he did it, right? Not prove that he didn't do it?"

"I don't think you're going to prove he didn't do it," Sara said. "Sheriff Pratt was here yesterday. More or less told me he just wants Lukas to wake up so he can haul him off to jail."

"Yeah, well, you'll get that," Drake muttered.

Rink snorted.

"What do you mean?" Sara asked.

Drake leaned back a moment, glanced around the deserted room. "To a cop, there's never any deeper meaning. No layers to dig through. No second gunman. There's the surface, and that's good enough."

"Especially a month after reelection, two days before Christmas," Rink added.

Sara nodded.

"Right," Drake said. "So again, we'll skip that. I understand your brother was in the service. Let's start there."

Another nod. "Lukas took a little bit different path than most. Coming out of high school, he had no intention of joining up. Couldn't imagine leaving Montana.

"At 18, he moved to Missoula, went to the U. Graduated with honors."

"Majoring in what?" Drake asked. Scribbled notes as she talked.

"Animal science. He wanted to come back and take over the ranch someday. Figure out the best way to breed our own stock instead of sending off for artificial insemination each year."

"So what happened?"

"Hard times," Sara said. Offered a wistful turn of her head. "This was in 2005. The economy hadn't really bounced back after 9/11. Cattle prices weren't near what they had been, what they should have been."

"So he went into the service?" Drake prompted.

Sara bobbed her head. "He knew the ranch couldn't afford to provide for all three of us, especially with his having student loans, so he enlisted."

"Army?"

"Yes. Because he came in with a degree, he started as a Corporal. Rose to a Staff Sergeant before leaving a couple weeks ago."

Drake's eyebrows rose. "A couple *weeks* ago?"

"Yeah," Sara said. Lowered her voice to little more than a whisper. "Papa took sick this fall. Pancreatic cancer. Nobody, not even him, knew about it."

"Damn," Drake muttered. Knew better than to say he was sorry.

He'd been in her position before.

It was the last thing she wanted to hear.

"Whole thing, from finding out to funeral, took two months. When Lukas first heard, he filed for a Compassionate Discharge."

Drake wrote the words down on his tablet and underlined them. He had no idea what they meant, but finding out would be easy enough.

He didn't want to interrupt the flow.

"To everybody's surprise, they were pretty cool about it. He'd already been in eight years, had a sparkling record. Since it was for family medical hardship, they granted his release.

"Even still, it is the Army. These things take time."

Drake stopped writing. Looked up at her. "Did he make it in time?"

Moisture formed in the corners of Sara's eyes. No tears fell.

"He did, but just barely. He got about three days with him before he went. I swear, Lukas coming home was the only thing that kept Papa going as long as he did."

Drake made another note to check the death records for an exact timeline. Again, he didn't want to stop the story on small details.

It was a problem, he found, most lawyers tended to battle.

Too much attention on the trees, not enough on the forest.

"Okay," Drake said. Leaned forward. Kept the pen poised before him. "Connect the dots here for me. How did Lukas get from your father's side to being here now?"

"I don't know," Sara said. Gave a shake of the head for emphasis. "The whole first week he was back we were tied up with the showing and the funeral. I mean *the whole thing*. I don't know how he did it.

"We were both in shock, but his was a whole different level."

"How so?" Drake asked.

"I lost my dad. He lost his *life*. Discharged from the Army. Left the desert. Flew back from the other side of the world. I can't even imagine what he was going through."

"He ever say anything to you about it?"

Another shake of the head. "No. Just kept asking if I was alright."

"Was there anybody he would have spoken to?"

"Nobody around here. I know he has to attend counseling sessions with the Army for a couple months. He might have said something to them."

"Counseling?" Drake asked. Made another notation. "For?"

Sara glanced to Rink. Back to Drake. "Nothing bad. I just think it's standard now for soldiers getting out."

Drake nodded. "Makes sense. Do you know where he was doing those?"

"I don't."

"I can find out," Rink inserted. First words he'd uttered in some time.

Drake looked to him. Let the confusion show on his face. Made another note to ask about it later.

"Okay. So let's move to the meeting the other night. Was there anybody there in particular that Lukas had animosity toward?"

Sara twisted her head again. "Not at all. Heck, he's been gone the last eight years. I don't even think he's kept up with any of those people."

"Has anything happened since he's been back? An ugly scene at the funeral or anything?"

"No. There wasn't but a few handfuls of people there. Mostly old-time ranchers Papa knew for years, couple of others like Rink here."

Once more Drake flicked his eyes to the side. Back to Sara.

Silence fell over the table.

Drake leaned back. Studied the notes in front of him.

On the opposite side, Sara fidgeted. Stared down at her hands.

Rink remained motionless.

"The newspaper said it was an Agriculture Commission meeting. What does that mean, exactly?"

"Good question," Sara said. "Papa always went, always came home steaming mad. Always said he didn't want me wasting my time with them."

Drake wrote the information down. "That should all be public record. Can't be hard to find. Was this the first one Lukas went to?"

"Far as I know."

A pair of orderlies shuffled in on the opposite side of the room. Both looked bleary-eyed, either on the front or back end of a long shift.

They didn't notice the trio seated in the corner, concerned with their own conversation.

Drake watched them disappear into the serving area. Looked over his notes once more. Glanced at the clock on the wall.

"Thank you again for meeting with me this morning. I will no doubt have a mountain of new questions soon enough, but this will get me started."

Sara and Rink both nodded.

"Tomorrow is Christmas, so I won't be able to get much done until Tuesday. Can we meet again Wednesday or Thursday to fill in any gaps I come across?"

"Sure," Sara said. Her voice was just above a whisper, void of anything resembling emotion.

"I'll contact you later with the information about his counseling," Rink added.

Drake glanced down at his notes. Thought about his previous trip to Hamilton the day before.

"Please do. Goslin will no doubt start there. I should too."

CHAPTER THIRTEEN

Steaming.

It was the first time in seven years Drake had seen Ajax warm in between the months of October and May. To his extreme surprise, his friend wasn't just tepid.

He wasn't even hot.

He was flat out steaming.

Drake could almost see it rolling off his dreadlocks as he tossed a duffel bag into the bed of the truck. Paused long enough to let Suzy Q jump in the cab. Climbed in after her.

If not for the fact that Drake knew how upset his friend really was, he might have cracked a smile.

Instead, he kept his face drawn tight. Put his own duffel bag into the bed. Slid in behind the wheel.

He pulled the truck out of their driveway and angled across town. Stayed off the freeway. Drove slow.

"What time do you get in tonight?"

"Too damn early."

A wince crossed Drake's face before he could think to stop it. "That bad?"

"Worse."

Drake slowed the truck a bit more. Pulled up short at a light just turning amber.

"Thanks," Ajax said. Stared out the window, anger rolling off him in waves.

Even Q sensed it, pressing herself tight against Drake's leg.

"I didn't realize things had gotten so bad..." Drake said. Let his voice trail off.

"They haven't," Ajax replied. "Not really, anyway. It's just...my mom's trying to play matchmaker again. Thinks it'll make me want to move back."

"Ouch."

"Pretty much."

"At Christmas?"

"Worse than that," Ajax said. "I just found out mom asked *her* to pick me up from the airport. Told her she was so swamped with getting things ready for the party..."

Drake had to bite his tongue to keep from smiling at his friend's demise. "That's cold. Explains the hostility, though."

Through his best efforts, Drake managed to extend the 12 minute drive to an even 20. Simple fact was though, it was still Missoula.

On Christmas Eve.

There was only so much stalling one could do.

He said goodbye to a grumbling Ajax on the curb by the front door of the airport. Pulled away from the same spot he'd used two days before with Ava and headed back into town.

Just minutes after 11:00, Drake came to a stop in front of the apartment the Keuhl's shared. Found Sage standing on the front steps.

Duffel bag on the ground to her left. Oversized paper bag of gifts to her right.

She bent at the waist as he climbed out. Lifted as much as she could from the ground. Left the rest behind for him.

"You're late."

"Blame Ajax," Drake said. Lifted Sage's duffel. Grunted. "You realize this is just for a couple days, right?"

"You realize I'm a girl, right?" Sage replied over her shoulder.

"What? Really? You?"

Sage ignored the retort. Loaded her bags into the truck. Stood by the passenger door as Drake circled to the opposite side.

Together they climbed in. Drake goosed the heat a little higher as Q greeted Sage with hot breath and sloppy kisses.

Sage was long past trying to fight it.

"So how'd it go this morning?"

"Can't you feel his hostility still lingering in here?"

"Now that you mention it, this spot does feel abnormally warm. That's not what I meant, though."

Drake nodded. He knew what she meant. Was hoping to dodge it until he'd had some more time to sort things out.

The hour-long ride from Hamilton had barely made a dent in the tangle in his head. He was a long way from making sense of everything still.

"Well?" Sage pressed.

Drake exhaled through his nose. Smiled. Turned the truck onto the highway and headed west.

"I'm still processing."

"Process out loud."

The words weren't a command. More like a statement of the obvious. Sage wanted to help. Drake often needed it.

"Lot of moving parts," Drake said. "The things that add up don't equal enough to explain what happened. The parts that don't fit are too big to be ignored."

"Start at the beginning," Sage said. Settled her hand down behind Q's ears. Kneaded the folds of skin in concentric circles.

A low, guttural moan rumbled from within Q, voicing her approval.

"Guy with a glowing service record finds out his father is dying and gets a special discharge to come home. Gets here, has less than a week, has to bury him."

"Oof," Sage said. Cringed.

"The funeral is small. Few old-timers, couple random friends. No problems or altercations. No trouble of any kind.

"Couple of days pass, he goes to the monthly Agriculture Commission meeting. Sits in for a while, apparently hears something he doesn't like, gets up and walks out.

"Nobody thinks much of it until he walks back in with a rifle."

"Just like the news said, huh?" Sage asked.

"Best I can tell," Drake said. "I haven't talked to any witnesses yet or anything. Just his sister, who wasn't there."

"Not quite an unbiased source."

"Looking at maybe losing her brother and father in a two-week stretch? Definitely not."

Silence fell for a moment. Drake stared out through the windshield at a slate-colored sky. Just one more in an unending string of The Greys.

Beside him, Sage sat with her face deep in thought. Chewed over what she'd just learned. Tried to fit some pieces together.

"Okay, so walk me through this. What does and doesn't fit?"

Drake rested his wrists atop the wheel. Brought his thumb and pinkie together to count things off.

"First, his service record. According to his sister, he was a model soldier. So much so, they let him walk mid-tour.

"Within a week of returning, he opens fire in a public place?"

"Post-traumatic stress? Traumatic brain injury?" Sage proffered.

"I don't know," Drake said. "He's required to meet with an Army shrink for the next few months. Rink is supposed to get back to me with who he was seeing."

"You going to go talk to them?"

"Hopefully on Tuesday, right after leaving your place."

Sage nodded. "Okay, so what doesn't make sense?"

Drake twisted his face. Pushed out a loud breath. "The guy was a sniper. Grew up hunting deer. You mean to tell me he walked into a crowded meeting hall, opened fire, and didn't hit *anybody*?"

The information brought a look of surprise to Sage's face. She leaned back. Raised her eyebrows. Stared at two young girls decorating a pine tree in their front yard outside.

"Yeah, that doesn't sound right."

"And on the other side," Drake continued. "The opening fire itself. What were they talking about at the meeting? What had him so pissed off?"

"Pissed enough to walk outside, get a gun, and come back in firing."

"Exactly. This is a local Agriculture Commission meeting. It's not like it was a Senate budget hearing."

The corner of Sage's mouth turned up into a half-smile. She lowered her face down to the top of Q's head. Felt the soft fur against her lips.

Thought about what they'd just discussed.

"Oh, I don't know. Some of the ranchers can get pretty worked up about things."

Drake slowed the truck. Turned north off the highway at French-town. Headed along 83 toward Arlee and the rez.

"But he's been gone eight years. What could they be talking about that would have him that mad, that fast?"

CHAPTER FOURTEEN

Delmonico.

Inch thick bone-in rib-eye steaks.

Beef raised right on the Bar-T ranch. Free range, grass fed.

Most families have ham on Christmas. Perhaps a turkey.

Not the Tierney's. Every year they slaughtered a prize steer for the occasion, removing ten Delmonico cuts.

One for Holt and his wife Bernice. One for each of the four sons and their wives.

In addition, they hand ground the remaining rib-eye meat into burgers for the six grandchildren.

All told it came out to almost 20 pounds of beef for the family.

Taken together with all the trimmings Bernice insisted on each year, it was enough to feed a small village. A veritable feast.

At the moment, that feast sat growing cold.

The smell of it permeated the house. Filled every last nook and cranny. Had the children whining on the front couch. Left their parents casting angry glances into the study.

Holt Tierney paid all of it no attention. Not even the delectable aroma of his favorite cut of meat in the entire world.

Instead, he sat perched on the edge of his desk. Inspected the pointed toe of his Roper. Ran his thumb and forefinger across his moustache one time after another.

Seated in front of him in the same chair that Johnson and McIlvaine had both used the afternoon before was his daughter-in-law Jessica.

To everyone else in the world, she was Jess.

To Holt, hellbent on formality, it was always Jessica.

She sat leaning forward in the chair, her legs crossed. A spiral bound Steno notepad was balanced on her knee. A tape recorder was active on the arm of the chair.

"Tell me, Mr. Tierney, what went through your mind as you saw the perpetrator enter the room, brandishing a weapon?"

Holt drew in a deep breath through his nose. Used the expansion of his lungs to lift his squared shoulders several inches higher. Held the pose a full moment.

Pushed it out in a slow, even pace.

"To be honest, I don't know that anything entered my mind. It all happened so fast, I didn't have a chance."

Jessica scribbled down his response.

As a contributing writer for *The Missoulian*, Jessica covered the odd story from Hamilton. Holt had approached her three days earlier with an idea for the piece.

Told her that several people around had asked for his story and he wanted her to have it.

Truth was, he wanted to get his side of things out while Webb was still in a coma. Solidify the version he and McIlvaine had agreed to before anybody could say otherwise.

The only reason he chose Jessica as his vessel was he knew she was scared to death of him. Wouldn't dream of challenging his telling.

Holt had never thought much of her work as a writer. The only one of his four daughter-in-laws that was gainfully employed, he tolerated it at best.

Loathed it at worst.

Nothing against her or her writing, more the idea of women working in general. It was the man's job to provide, just as he had for Bernice over the years.

"Would you say his actions were in any way provoked?"

"Certainly not," Holt replied. Continued stroking his moustache. Shook his head for emphasis.

"In fact, it was the first time I had even seen the young man in, well, must be close to a decade."

"I understand he just returned from serving in the Army?"

"That is my understanding as well, a most noble service that we are all thankful for."

Jessica continued to transcribe his words. Paused to turn the page. Wrote some more.

"Were you familiar with the young man's father that recently passed?"

"Of course," Holt said. Nodded. "Everybody in Hamilton knew Mitch Webb. A true genuine-article rancher. A great loss to the community."

"Ever any hostility between Mr. Webb and yourself? Or anybody on the commission?"

Holt leaned back. Paused. Ran a hand over his wiry grey hair.

"You know, I can't say that I ever knew Mitch to have hostility with anybody, about anything."

"So this really was just an isolated incident? Out of the blue?"

"It certainly seems that way," Holt said. "I've replayed those events in my mind a dozen times, cannot think of a single reason why he acted the way he did."

Jessica nodded, her straight brown hair falling on either side of her shoulders. She sat with her mouth pursed, writing as fast as her hand would allow.

"Now, the man that was able to stop Mr. Webb's rampage is an employee of yours, is that correct?"

"Yes, he is," Holt said. "Hank McIlvaine was recently hired on here as a consultant. He was sitting in on the meeting at my request."

"And when the shooting started...?" Jessica asked. Let her voice trail off.

"Mr. McIlvaine is retired from the United States Marine Corps and has had a concealed carry permit since his discharge 13 years ago. All of us there that night were very fortunate he was present and acted so quickly."

"Have you reached out to the Webb family at all since the incident?"

Holt pulled his chin back toward his chest. Folded his arms. Peered down his nose at his daughter-in-law.

"I have wanted to do so, but was requested by local law enforcement not to until after their investigation."

Jessica nodded. Finished the sentence she was writing.

"And one last question, has this incident affected anything for the local ranching community moving forward?"

"Certainly not," Holt said. Forced a smile onto his face so large it hurt. "In fact, as a gesture to prove as much, I would like to remind everyone that our annual Winter Ball is still planned for next weekend here at the ranch. The entire community is invited for a night of dining and dancing."

Jessica smiled as she wrote. Nodded her head in agreement at the statement.

Once she was done, she raised her eyes to him. Flipped the notepad closed.

"I think that's everything. Was there anything else you wanted to add?"

"No, that about covers it," Holt said. Beamed at her. Leaned forward and clasped her hands in his. "Thank you so much for doing this. You were perfect."

"My pleasure. I talked to my editor this morning, he said it should run Tuesday. Wednesday at the latest," Jessica responded. Stood. "Now, should we get in there? It sounds like the crowd might be getting a bit restless."

Holt kept the smile in place.

"You go on ahead. I'll be right behind you in just a minute."

Jessica nodded and turned for the door. Headed out, nudging it almost closed behind her.

Holt waited until the back of her black dress was gone from sight before circling around the desk. Lifting the phone receiver. Pressing it to his face.

Taking it off of speakerphone.

"You get all that?"

"Consultant, huh?" McIlvaine asked. A trace of sarcasm in his voice. A bit of bemusement as well.

"What the hell would you like me to call you? Hired gun?" Holt spat.

"Naw, consultant works."

"Good, because until this thing blows over, that's what your job title is going to be. I'm even having business cards printed up that say just that."

"You really think all this is necessary?" McIlvaine asked. "Staged interviews? Fake business cards?"

"Yes it is necessary, you idiot," Holt snapped. "Paula Goslin herself told you last night that the Webb's have hired an attorney. That means they're looking into things."

Silence fell for a moment. Stayed long enough that Holt pulled the phone away to make sure the connection hadn't been lost.

"McIlvaine? You there?"

"There are easier ways to make sure they don't find anything, you know."

Holt sighed. Raised his gaze to the six-by-six elk on the wall he harvested two winters before. Shook his head.

"And you know why that bastard started shooting in the first place, don't you? This is a lot bigger than just some lawyer snooping around or a couple of shots fired in a meeting.

"We need to make sure people keep looking everywhere but at us."

"And if they do?"

"We need to make sure they don't."

"So what do you want me to do?" McIlvaine asked.

There was a pause as Holt lowered his head back to eye level. Shook it from side to side.

"Nothing. Yet."

"Alright," McIlvaine said. "You're the boss."

Holt grunted in agreement.

"Merry Christmas," McIlvaine said. Cut the call off without another word.

Holt held the phone in his hand a moment. Lowered it back to its cradle.

"Yeah. Something like that."

CHAPTER FIFTEEN

Drake was miserable.

Painfully, woefully, miserably, full.

There was no possible way his body could hold even one more bite.

Kristina Keuhl, matron saint of the Keuhl family, didn't seem to care. She brushed off his repeated requests for reprieve. Brought him one plate after another from the kitchen.

Smiled each time he implored her to stop. Told him to quit being polite.

It was Christmas. He was family.

Technically, this wasn't even the holiday feast. That would come on Christmas Day. This was a mother happy to have hungry mouths around to feed.

She wasn't about to let the opportunity pass her by, even long after they ceased being hungry.

Drake sat sprawled across an overstuffed arm chair in the corner, his stomach bulged in front of him. Suzy Q lay belly-up on the floor at his feet.

Kristina's force feeding didn't differentiate between man and beast.

Across from him, Sage and Kade were on either end of the couch, both slouched toward their respective corners.

Each looked even more miserable than he did.

Perched at the far end of the room in his recliner was Wes Keuhl, patriarch of the clan. The Sunday paper was folded into quarters and rested on his knee, the crossword puzzle staring up at him.

In his late 50s, he had the look of an athlete gone to seed. Thick arms and shoulders. Square jaw. A growing paunch. Thinning auburn hair.

A pair of bifocals rested on the tip of his nose as he stared down at the paper. Seemed to ignore the ritual gluttony occurring around him.

To Drake's immediate left was a brick fireplace. The cast iron doors on it stood open, a metal mesh screen pulled across the front. The smell of hickory wood filled the air.

Warmth spilled out in a wide arc.

Above it, a college football game that nobody was watching was on television.

In the corner, a faux pine tree was covered in gaudy decorations. Oversized bulbs bathed the room in hues of red and green.

"Well now, how about some dessert?" Katrina asked. Swept into the room. Wrung her hands on her apron. Stood with fists resting on her hips.

The question brought a smile to Drake's lips. He raised his arm to his face. Used the crook of his elbow to shield his eyes.

Shook his head.

"Mom, I don't think any of us could even consider eating more right now," Sage said. Made no attempt to hide her discomfort.

"What, you guys didn't like it?" Katrina asked, voice tinged with sadness.

Drake dropped the arm from his face. Kept the smile and the head shake. Looked over at Kade, making the same expression.

"Yes, mom, that's what we're saying," Kade said. "Not that we're all so full we might puke at any moment. We didn't like it."

Katrina made a face. Stood in place and looked at each of them.

Unlike her husband, who was of Germanic descent, Katrina was a local product. Full-blooded Salish Indian. Long blue-black hair. Pointed chin and cheekbones. Dark complexion.

One at a time she looked to her children and Drake, hoping someone would take her up on dessert.

Nobody did.

Pouting, she turned and huffed toward the kitchen. No doubt on a mission to prepare for the next day.

"You're getting soft," Sage said. Aimed her gaze at Drake. "Wasn't that long ago you would have eaten at least two, three more plates without blinking."

"You see how many meatballs I took down?" Drake countered. "I lost track somewhere in the 20s."

"I don't think the ones you were slipping Q count, you know," Sage replied.

Drake smiled. Rested his head back against the chair.

"Q didn't get any meatballs. Some smoked trout maybe, but no meatballs."

The comment spurred life from the easy chair, Wes twisting his paper to the side to peer at Drake.

"You gave that dog my trout?"

Q moaned in response before Drake could respond. The combined laughter of Kade and Sage made it impossible for him to even try.

Drake leaned back in his chair. Returned his arm to cover his eyes. Felt his phone vibrate against his hip.

With his off-hand he fished it out and held it at arm's length. Peered beneath his bicep to check the caller ID.

Let his arm fall away and stood.

"Yeah, that's what I thought," Wes said. Returned to the crossword. Drew more laughter from his progeny.

Still smiling, Drake wagged the phone at the room. Excused himself.

"Uh-huh, run away," Kade taunted.

"Go get some more meatballs," Sage called.

Drake continued to shake his head. Exited into the adjacent dining room, already set up in anticipation of the morrow's meal.

A red table cloth covered an expansive cherry wood table. Gold-rimmed plates sat in front of five chairs. Water glasses were polished clean, silverware already in place.

Drake walked past it to the windows overlooking the front lawn. Stared out at a thin blanket of snow being whipped around by the wind.

Raised the phone to his face.

"Hello?"

"I got the information you needed," Rink said. No salutation. No lead-in.

Drake hadn't expected there to be.

There never was.

"Okay."

"Sorry to call so late. It took me a while to track it down."

Rink never apologized either. For him to do so now meant Sara must be close by.

"How's Lukas doing?"

"No change," Rink said. "Stable, but..." He let the statement drift off. Didn't want to say the word coma aloud.

Drake nodded toward the window. "And Sara?"

"Exactly the same."

Drake nodded again. He knew the feeling. Like standing on the outside, watching your own body go through the motions.

"Again, you're welcome to come here," Drake said. Even though it wasn't his place to extend the invite, the Keuhl's had done as much repeatedly over the course of the afternoon.

If he didn't make the offer, there'd be hell to pay.

Besides, maybe two more mouths would be able to keep up with Kristina's prodigious output.

Drake doubted it, but wouldn't turn away the help.

"Thank you - all of you - but we're not going anywhere."

There was no doubt from the tone that the decision was final. It wasn't hostile, but it wasn't negotiable.

"Okay," Drake said. Conceded the point. "So, what were you able to find out?"

"I shook the bushes a little bit and found out all psychiatric evaluations are done through Fort Harrison in Helena."

"I've been by there. Those will be sealed medical records, but I'll call first thing Tuesday and see what I can find."

"I can do you one better. The lady you want to speak with is a Dr.-," there was a pause as Rink checked the name, "Cheryl Woodson. She's expecting you at 11:00."

Drake's eyebrows rose a half-inch on his forehead. A puff of air slipped from his lips.

"That a problem?" Rink asked. "Sorry, I know I should have checked with you first."

"No, that's fine," Drake said. "I was just thinking, that was some bush you shook to pull all that off, on Christmas Eve no less."

"It was," Rink affirmed. "Might have even had a few stars on its shoulder."

"Damn. There are two-star generals living in Hamilton?"

"I didn't say two stars, or Hamilton," Rink said. Another hint of finality.

Drake's eyebrows rose a little higher, but he let it pass.

"So 11:00, Cheryl Woodson," Drake said, shifting the subject.

"Yeah, just go to the front gate and ask to speak with her, they'll tell you where to go."

"I'll be there. Thanks a lot, man."

"Thank you," Rink replied. "Let me know if anything comes loose I might be able to help with."

"Will do. Merry Christmas, to you and Sara both."

"Thanks, same to you," Rink said. Hung up.

Drake stared another moment out the window. Watched as the top of a pair of Lodge Pole Pines in the front yard bent beneath the wind.

Had his attention drawn away by the reflection of Sage approaching in the glass.

"Get done talking to your girlfriend?" Sage asked. Arched an eyebrow.

"Sure did. Rink says hi."

The eyebrow fell into a half-smile. "Sara?"

Drake smiled. Should have known Sage would be listening.

"The sister. He's there at the hospital with her."

"Are they...?"

Drake shook his head. "I'm not sure. I know enquiring minds would like to know, so I'll ask at some point. Just haven't had a chance yet."

"Much appreciated," Sage said. Bowed the top of her head.

Drake circled around the table. Headed back toward his place in the corner.

"Cheryl Woodson?" Sage asked.
"Lukas Webb's psychiatrist."
Sage nodded. Said nothing.

CHAPTER SIXTEEN

Boxing Day.

An English holiday demarcating the day after Christmas. A day when employers, masters, would bestow gifts upon their servants. Everything placed in a single box.

In the United States, it is a bit more somber.

The day after Christmas. A time when people are either feeling the post-holiday hangover, fighting to return an ill-gotten gift, or dragging themselves back to work.

Drake fell into the third category.

He rose in time with the sun and bade the Keuhl's thanks many, many times over. Accepted a bag of food for the road from Kristina that would keep he and Q both fed for much of the week.

Bumped fists with Kade on his way out.

Gave Sage a hug.

By 7:00 a.m. he and Q were back on the road, headed south. With luck, most of the reservation was still asleep, the roads empty as he drove. Already the merriment of the previous days was gone from mind, thoughts of where he was going occupying his thoughts.

A light wind blew west-to-east across the highway beneath his tires. Pushed a spray of white powder over the blacktop. Did nothing to slow his progress as he reached Interstate 90 and turned east toward Missoula.

A quick pit stop by the house allowed him to change clothes, drop off Q, leave his duffel on the floor. Less than 20 minutes after arriving he was back on the road, dressed in slacks and a sweater.

The world around him was starting to come alive as he slipped out of Missoula and headed toward Helena. The sun, nothing more than a thin white disc, rose above the horizon. Cars dotted the interstate.

Drake paid them no mind as he drove into the morning. Kept the radio off and the heater on high.

One by one, he gnawed at the fingernails on his left hand. Tried to get his jaw to keep pace with the frenetic interworking of his mind.

Failed miserably.

An hour after leaving home, Drake nudged his truck off the interstate. Headed north up State Route 12. Had the road to himself as he pushed out the last 60 miles into the state capitol.

Gone were the open tracts of land from the interstate, the meandering Clark Fork River. In their place was farm country. Rolling fields of clover and alfalfa. Scattered bunches of cattle, Black Angus and Brown Baldies.

Stretches of undisturbed snow.

Drake inventoried the questions he wanted to ask in his mind as he went. Found Fort Harrison two miles shy of Helena proper.

Pulled up to the front gate 15 minutes before 11:00.

A guard that looked to be just a day over 18 waited for Drake to pull even with the patrol booth before stepping outside.

"Morning," the young man grumbled, cheeks and ears both bright red with cold.

"Good morning. Drake Bell, here to see Dr. Cheryl Woodson."

The young man glared at Drake. Looked down at the clipboard in his hand. Peeled back a top sheet and continued to read in silence.

"Dr. Woodson is in back at the hospital. Follow this road until it T's out, turn right. Visitor parking is out front."

He turned and headed back without waiting for a response.

"Thank you," Drake said to the back of his head. Rolled his window up. Pushed the blower on the heater a little higher.

Drake followed the directions given to him and pulled up in front of the VA Montana Health Care System 10 minutes before the hour. He parked in a space marked by blue paint.

No other cars in the visitor stalls.

Threw his bag over his shoulder. Shuffled inside as fast as he could without running.

The atmosphere was subdued as he stepped through the set of double doors and stood in a wide foyer of polished white tile. Looked from side to side in an attempt to get his bearings.

Another guard, a carbon copy of the first save for his black hair to the front gate's brown, stared from behind the front desk. Looked bored. Waited for Drake to approach him.

"Hi, I have an appointment with Dr. Cheryl Woodson."

The man looked at Drake a moment. Narrowed his eyes.

"Active duty is across the street. This facility is for veteran's only."

A look of confusion passed over Drake's face. Faded as he thought of his shorn hair.

"I'm neither. I'm a lawyer representing a recently discharged Army Ranger."

The guard's eyes narrowed a bit further. He let the gaze linger a second longer than necessary before lowering it to a chart on the desk before him.

"Room 321. Elevators are down the hall."

"Thanks," Drake mumbled. Set off before having to interact with him any further.

The elevator deposited him on the third floor, a desolate stretch of gleaming white. Drake stood a moment and looked in either direction. Started walking to the right.

Realized the numbers were going in the wrong direction. Went back the opposite way.

He found room 321 four minutes before 11:00. Door closed. No light on beneath it.

Rapped on it with the back of his hand. Didn't get a response.

On the far end of the hallway, a janitor shuffled into view. Drake watched him a moment. Turned back to the door. Knocked again.

Still no response.

Drake removed his cellphone and checked the time.

One minute before 11:00.

He considered texting Rink and making sure he was where he was supposed to be. Reasoned with himself that both guards wouldn't have let him through unless things checked out.

The sound of the janitor grew closer, his feet shuffling across the floor.

Drake turned toward the old man with tufts of white sprouting from the top of his head and each of his ears. Watched him push a broom forward without any real regard for what he was doing.

"Good morning," Drake said. Smiled. Raised his chin in greeting.

The janitor kept moving like he wasn't there. Didn't respond in any way. Remained stooped over his implement, gaze aimed at the ground.

Kept the broom aimed in a straight line. Marched it right past Drake.

As he went, his left hand reached into the shirt pocket of his uniform. Produced a single folded white card. Extended it between his thumb and forefinger toward Drake.

Drake accepted the card. Mumbled a thank you.

Made no attempt to hide the confusion on his face.

Not once did the janitor break stride as he went.

Pushed the broom to the end of the hall and rounded a corner. Disappeared from view without ever saying a word.

Drake waited until he was gone before opening the card and staring down at it.

Allowed the look of confusion to further cloud his features.

A single line, written in a woman's hand.

Café Zydeco. As soon as you can get here.

CHAPTER SEVENTEEN

Eleven minutes.

That's all it took for Drake to make it back to his truck and drive the short distance into town.

He ignored inquisitive stares from both guards as he went. Set his face in a scowl that told them both he wasn't to be questioned.

Not that he was actually angry, he just didn't want to be stopped. All they would do is ask a bunch of questions he had no idea how to answer.

Making the first right he came to, Drake pulled into the parking lot for Café Zydeco. Turned the truck off and sat staring straight ahead.

The entire structure was little more than a coffee hut. Maybe 15 feet in length. Not even that long in width.

No way could it hold more than a quartet of tables.

Drake watched as a pair of middle-aged ladies walked outside with white paper bags under their arms. Powerwalked to a Prius. Climbed inside and drove away without once looking his direction.

With a heavy sigh, Drake grabbed up his bag from the seat beside him. Wrenched the door open and headed inside. For the first time all morning, didn't notice the Arctic blast blowing across his body.

Not that he was hostile. Just, intensely curious.

A small bell announced his arrival to the restaurant. A trio of stares turned as he entered. Two belonged to girls in their early 20s working behind the counter. No doubt college students helping out over break.

Drew the short straw on the day after Christmas.

The third belonged to a woman in her early-30s. Couldn't have been more than a half-dozen years older than Drake.

Short blonde hair tucked behind her ears. Blue eyes. Yoga pants and a fleece pullover.

Her gaze met his as he entered and she nodded once.

Drake took the cue and walked toward her. Extended his hand out before him.

"Dr. Woodson?"

"Cherie, please. Mr...?" she asked, returned his handshake.

Firm. Warm.

"Drake."

"Alright, Mr. Drake. Please, join me."

Drake pulled out the chair across from her. Slid down into it. "No, first name Drake."

Cherie nodded as one of the girls walked to the table. A strawberry blonde ponytail swung to either side as she approached. Oversized smile aimed at Drake.

"Can I get you something?"

Drake opened his mouth to decline. Turned to Cherie.

"Are you having anything?"

"Cajun turkey sandwich," Cherie responded. Offered a sheepish smile.

"Same," Drake said to the waitress. "And a sweet tea if you've got it."

"Alright," the girl responded. Somehow managed to spread her smile even wider.

Drake waited for her to head back behind the counter before returning his attention to Cherie. She sat staring back at him, seeming to size him up.

He couldn't help but smile.

"I'm not what you expected," Drake said.

"No," Cherie replied. "Can't imagine I'm what you thought you were meeting today either, though."

"No," Drake conceded. "Though that's not at the top of my list of questions right now."

The same sheepish smile crossed Cherie's face. "Yeah, sorry about that. I got a call this morning informing me it would be better if this conversation was held off-site."

"And off the record?"

Cherie's eyebrows rose. "Did you get a similar call?"

"No, but it's not hard to put together. The way this whole thing came about. You sitting here alone. It makes sense."

Mock surprise crossed Cherie's face. "Can't a girl just be in the mood for a turkey sandwich?"

"The day after Christmas? You've probably got more turkey at home than you know what to do with."

The remark brought a snort from Cherie. "Ham, actually. But the general sentiment isn't wrong."

"So then why are we here?" Drake asked. "This feels a lot more like hiding out than having a real conversation about Lukas Webb's health."

"It is and it isn't," Cherie said. "I'm not worried about anybody hearing anything. It's just that inside the walls of the VA Medical Center, in my official capacity, I'm quite constrained about what I can and can't say.

"Out here, I'm just having lunch with a new friend. If we happen to be talking about work and something comes up, so be it."

Drake leaned back from the table. Blew out a sigh. Swung his gaze around the room.

He had overestimated the place from the outside. The counter and service prep areas were larger than expected.

It left just enough room for two tables.

"I have no idea who called in this favor, but they must have had some clout."

"Retired or not," Cherie said, "A four-star general is a four-star general."

There was no attempt by Drake to hide the surprise on his face.

"Wow. Impressive. Dare I ask what he went to the trouble of having you here to tell me?"

"By all means," Cherie replied. Motioned with a hand across the table. "I am here to tell you absolutely nothing."

Drake's jaw dropped open. He twisted his head to the side to look at her. "Come again?"

A smile crossed Cherie's features. "Allow me to rephrase. I'm not here to tell you I refuse to speak. I'm here to tell you, there's nothing to tell."

Drake could feel his brow furrowing. "Wait, seriously?"

"Seriously," Cherie said. Nodded once for emphasis. "That guy was one of the most well-adjusted soldiers I've ever come across. If not for his father taking ill, he would have been a lifer.

"And a good one at that."

Confusion continued to play across Drake's features. Kept the words in his mind from finding his mouth.

"I know," Cherie said. "I'm sure you've seen all the stuff on the news, in the papers, about Post Traumatic Stress, about Traumatic Brain Injury.

"And believe me, those things exist and are very serious. Everything you've heard is true, times a thousand."

"But not Lukas Webb?"

"But not Lukas Webb," Cherie echoed.

"He just returned a few weeks ago, though. How many times have you been able to meet with him?"

"Three times. We were scheduled for a total of eight, but before this happened, I was going to cancel the remaining sessions.

"He was good, just wanted to get on with his life."

Drake ran a hand over his face and leaned back in his chair. Looked behind the counter where the two girls built his sandwich.

"You look shell-shocked," Cherie said.

This time, the sheepish smile was his.

"That obvious?"

"I *am* a trained psychiatrist."

Drake raised his eyes in concession. "It's just, I came over here with a whole slate of questions to ask you, but none of them seem very relevant at the moment."

"I figured as much," Cherie said. "That's part of why I wanted to meet you here. It's much easier for me to be blunt than in the office."

"Yeah? Did you have to pull the cloak-and-dagger thing with the janitor too?"

A laugh burst out of Cherie, followed by her hands covering her mouth. "Herb pulled the old Silent Messenger routine again, huh? I swear he lives for that sort of stuff."

"He's pretty convincing at it."

Cherie smiled and shook her head. Said nothing.

Drake smiled for a moment as well. Let it fade as he worked to process her words.

"You're being on the up-and-up with me here, right? His family has retained me as his lawyer. I know medical records are protected under patient-doctor confidentiality, but it would help me tremendously to see what kind of mental stress he was under at the time of the incident."

"Better for both of us to avoid a court order."

Cherie spread her hands out in front of her. Shook her head from side to side.

"Look, I wish there was more I could tell you, I really do. Truth is, I'm just as stumped as you are. Lukas Webb had a glowing service record and clean bill of health."

"And there's no way he could have hidden something from you? Slipped it by somehow?"

A momentary cloud passed by Cherie's eyes.

"Every week I see somewhere between 50 and 100 soldiers. Some are fresh off the boat from foreign soil. Some have been retired for 20 years.

"I have seen every ailment - physical and mental - that a man can go through. Believe me, if he was hiding something, he deserves an Oscar for his performance."

The words rested with finality between them a moment. There was no mistaking the bit of venom laced throughout.

"I meant no disrespect," Drake said. "Just trying to figure out how this could have happened."

Cherie stared at him a moment. Allowed the fire to dim behind her gaze.

"Sorry. It's just, since the shooting, I've been going over things in my mind on loop, trying to figure out if I missed something. Why he did it."

"Any insights you'd like to share?" Drake asked.

A slow, sad head shake was Cherie's response.

"All I can tell you is, whatever reason he had for doing it wasn't connected to his time in the service. That boy's mind was right.

"If he walked into a room and opened fire that night, it's because they damned well deserved it."

CHAPTER EIGHTEEN

There was a time when Holt Tierney oversaw every aspect of the ranch himself.

Payables. Shipping and receiving. Vaccinations. Branding.

Everything.

Over the years, one by one he had relinquished control of bits and pieces.

Payroll was the first to go. Followed soon thereafter by billing. Then shipping.

Age and success combined to push him to the fringe of his own operation. He was no longer the man with his hands on the reins.

Instead, he became the man holding the purse strings.

Just 15 minutes into his ride, Holt could already feel his backside starting to knot up. A lifetime spent in the saddle had turned his pelvis and lower back into a piece of driftwood.

Twisted sinew, dried and hardened into place.

It didn't take long for the old aches to come running back. Remind him why he had started handing off tasks in the first place.

Despite his physical discomfort, this morning it was a necessary evil. He had given the ranch hands an extra paid day off under the guise of a Christmas bonus. Told them all to enjoy it with their families.

Not to even think of returning until Wednesday morning.

Every last one had accepted the bit of good fortune without question. Even marveled to one another at how the old man was softening in his old age.

No one suspected it was because he wanted them all away for the day.

This was the closest thing to a covert operation a rancher would ever perform. He didn't need any extra eyes around to see it.

Just after lunch, Holt rose from the table and told Bernice he was going for a ride. Long familiar with his pains, the news surprised her, drawing token opposition.

Holt squelched it without much trouble.

Even managed to do so without having to resort to misogyny.

Dressed in work jeans, flannel, fleece vest and overcoat, he smashed a battered grey Justin cowboy hat down on his head. Went to the barn and saddled up.

Amanaka, his favorite trail horse from a lifetime together, was more willing than he was for the ride. An Appaloosa standing 12 hands high, she took the lead from pure muscle memory. Carried him down the trail without having to even think about it.

It was the exact reason Holt had always favored her, even now despite her age. Sure-footed and even tempered, never once had she spooked. Tried to buck him. Ever disagreed with his commands.

The smell of winter filled Holt's nostrils as they walked along. Pine needles dropping to the ground. Icy crystals whipping in the air. Fresh cow manure.

The afternoon was cold and still. Weak sun reflected off the snow.

The only sound was Amanaka's hooves crunching over the frozen ground.

Holt took the ride slow and easy until he was out of sight of the house. In the off chance Bernice was watching, or anybody else stopped by, he didn't want to raise suspicion.

The moment they crested a ridge and dropped from sight, he nudged Amanaka with his heels. Pushed her up to a light jog. Set a course through the back fields.

A half hour after leaving the house, he found what he was looking for.

Crouched in the back pasture was a small barn. Low-slung and without paint, the building itself was barely noticeable against the forest behind it.

What did stand out was the cluster of cows gathered tight. Large black blobs that came into focus the closer Holt drew.

Holt pulled Amanaka back to a walk and approached from the east. Swung out around the side of the barn.

Nodded as he saw a faded Ford Bronco parked out front.

"Right on time."

He rode on to the corner of the barn and slid down from the saddle, a practiced move he'd done a thousand times before.

Winced as his feet hit the ground.

Holt tied Amanaka up to the post out front and headed inside to find a large bear of a man already at work.

Brent Greeley stood as Holt entered, nodded. At full height, he was exactly between 6' and 7' tall. He weighed north of 300 pounds. Wore jeans with just a 38" waist.

Forty years ago, his enormous bulk made him an All-American for the Griz. Even made him a fair bit of money blocking for the Kansas City Chiefs.

In the time since, it made his life as a large-animal veterinarian much easier.

"Holt."

Holt walked across the straw-covered floor of the barn. Extended a hand. "Thank you for coming."

"Friendship doesn't end with retirement."

Holt nodded. Sensed a bit of gravity on the big man's features.

"Sorry I'm late, had to go slow to make sure Bernice didn't get suspicious."

Greeley nodded. "She doesn't know?"

"No," Holt replied. Shook his head. "I hate like hell hiding it from her, but we can't take any risks right now."

"Does anybody know?"

"Just you, me, and McIlvaine."

Greeley nodded again. Turned back to his work.

On the ground at his feet was spread a tarp several feet square. Atop it were over a dozen small vials. All were filled with a milky solution, mixtures of red and white.

A cardboard box holding row after row of clear vials sat off to the side.

A second box of unopened syringes sat beside it.

"How many have you gotten through so far?" Holt asked.

"Fifteen," Greeley replied. Flicked at the end of a syringe with his finger. Nudged a single drop of blood out with the plunger.

Inserted the needle into another vial. Pushed 10 cc's of blood into it.

He and Holt both watched as the blood swirled into the vial. The contents became cloudy, ribbons of red still visible.

"Any news yet?" Holt asked. Kept his gaze aimed at the vial.

"Not yet," Greeley replied. "It takes up to 20 minutes for the organisms to agglutinate. Won't know anything until then."

Holt grunted. Watched as Greeley put the vial down with the others.

"Looks like we've got 50 head outside," Greeley said. "How many you got total?"

"About 5,000."

"So that's 1% right here," Greeley said. Nodded. "Awful small sample. You think that'll be enough to do it?"

Holt shook his head. "It'll have to be."

Another nod was the only response.

Greeley bent at the waist and scooped out a handful of syringes. Extended a small clump to Holt. Extracted a black Sharpie from his back pocket and extended that as well.

"You start on one end, I'll keep working on the other?"

"Sounds good," Holt agreed.

"We need to draw out around 10 cc's. Best way is to grab up a handful of the skin behind their neck and go right in."

Holt nodded. He'd drawn enough blood from cows over the years to know the procedure.

Still, Greeley was doing him a favor. He wasn't about to act ungrateful.

"When you're done, be sure to mark the syringe with their tag number in case we do find anything."

"Got it," Holt said. Took the syringes. Split off in the opposite direction of Greeley and began drawing blood.

One at a time, the two men worked their way inward. Every 10 minutes or so, one of them would make a trip for more syringes. Drop off the ones they had used.

Each time he returned, Greeley inserted the drawn blood into the vials. Laid them out in careful rows atop the tarp.

The entire process took just over a half hour. Both men moved methodically, saying nothing.

Despite the cold, Holt could feel sweat start to form in the small of his back. Beneath his moustache.

He ignored it as he worked on, his mind racing, trying to piece together what would happen if one of the vials showed positive.

If more than one tested positive.

Once they were completed, both men stood in silence. Stared down at the samples lined up.

Greeley hung an oversized spotlight from an exposed beam overhead. Flipped it on. Squinted as harsh fluorescent light bathed the room.

Waited long enough to let his eyes adjust before checking his watch and starting with the first samples he'd drawn.

Moving slow, he lifted the vials and inspected them under the light. Content that a sample was negative, he marked it with his pen. Moved on to the next one.

Holt watched through the first handful before walking to the edge of the barn. Resting his boots on the bottom rung of fence. Leaning his elbows against the top.

A lone heifer spotted him and ambled over. Nudged the tips of his fingers hanging down with her nose. Licked at the remains of fried chicken grease from lunch on his fingertips.

A smile traced his lips as he watched her. Felt her tongue rub like medium-grit sandpaper against his skin. Smelled her hot breath in the space between them.

The moment was short lived.

"Hey, Holt," Greeley called.

Holt's eyes slid shut as he ignored the heifer, turned.

"Yeah?"

93

Greeley held up a single vial, the small glass implement appearing tiny in his massive paw.

Even from where he stood, Holt could see puffy red globules floating through the viscous liquid.

"We've got another one," Greeley said. No tone or inflection at all in his voice. Nothing more than a matter-of-fact statement.

The information hit Holt like a shot to the solar plexus.

Still, he fought to remain impassive.

"Just the one?"

"One," Greeley said. Nodded. "But this is an awful small sample size."

"Yeah."

Greeley lowered the vial back into position. "Number 393."

Holt nodded.

"Any idea where it's coming from?" Greeley asked.

"No."

"Any idea what you're going to do with it?"

Holt stared at the vial lying alongside the others and nodded.

Said nothing.

CHAPTER NINETEEN

Rink was waiting by his truck as Drake pulled up.

He didn't even come to a complete stop before Rink wrenched the door open. Climbed inside and slammed it shut.

Gave no indication that he'd even noticed the cold outside.

"Thanks for setting this up," Drake said.

"Thanks for everything you're doing," Rink responded.

Drake nodded. "Where to?"

"South through town, left on Bear Run Road."

The county seat of Ravalli County, Hamilton was home to right at 4,500 people. Most of them worked one of three places. The hospital. The sawmill. The local ranches.

Drake nosed the truck south. Past the Dairy Queen. Past Hamilton High School.

Small shops and boutiques lined the streets of downtown, the truck passing through almost as fast as it had entered. Just six minutes after leaving the hospital, they were headed west on Bear Run.

"Stay on this for about five miles. I'll point out the place when we get there."

"Alright," Drake said. "So what are we walking into again?"

Rink lifted a mesh ball cap from his head. Ran a hand back over his hair.

"I wouldn't say we're walking into anything. They'll treat you just fine, same as they did me a couple days."

"*They* being?"

A long sigh slid from Rink. "They call themselves the Home Guard. All former military. The place we're going is a little hole-in-the-wall where they gather."

"So, militia?" Drake asked.

"No," Rink said. Glanced to Drake. Shook his head. "Most true militia are anarchists. Hate the government, want to be left alone.

"These guys love America, support the government..."

"They just have serious misgivings about the direction both are headed," Drake finished.

"There you go," Rink said.

Drake drew in a deep breath. Watched as a coyote emerged from the woods up ahead and ran parallel to the road. Darted back into the brush without so much as glancing at them.

"How do you know about them?" Drake asked. "You were never in the military."

"No," Rink agreed. "A couple of them stopped by the hospital a few nights ago to visit Lukas. They'd heard on the news what had happened, wanted to pass along their support to the family."

"And you were there."

Rink nodded. "I was. It was late, maybe 2:00 or 3:00 in the morning. Sara was asleep in the chair, but I stepped outside and we talked a bit. They told me where to find them."

Drake nodded. Processed the information. "And they were okay with you being there?"

Rink's eyebrows rose. He looked out the window. "I don't know that I'd say okay, but they conceded it, since I was looking to help."

"What did Sara say about us going here?"

"Not a fan. At all," Rink said. Dropped his voice a bit lower. "But she's conceding it for the sake of her brother."

Drake nodded. Kept his attention aimed at the road.

Outside, the world was an exact replica of every day from the month before. His body still wasn't quite used to the bitter cold, but it was growing familiar with the monotony of the winter landscape.

Grey skies. Early nightfall. Temperatures that never crept above 30.

Wind that refused to stopped blowing.

"If you don't mind my asking..." Drake said.

"Lukas coached me," Rink said. Tossed the answer out before the question was fully asked.

Drake suspected he'd been expecting it.

"Was the head guy the entire time he was in college. My coach the full length of my career. When he went off to the Army, I took over for him."

The story made sense, though Drake felt there might be something he was leaving out.

"Good guy, I take it?"

"Very," Rink said. "The Crew would have – *will* - like him, when he's come through this."

Drake nodded. Debated offering some words of support. Decided against it.

Rink was never one to need it.

"So, you and Sara...?" Drake started.

His question was cut off by Rink pointing at a rusted metal mailbox. "Turn here."

Drake let it drop and turned in. Took his foot off the gas and allowed the truck to idle down a narrow two-track lane.

Branches pushed in tight from either side. Could be heard smacking against the truck.

They drove on in silence for two full minutes before the trees opened up. Gave way to a wooden outpost 30' square. Painted dark brown. Windows blacked out.

A tendril of smoke rising out of the chimney was the only sign of life from the building.

A handful of aged pickup trucks sat silent out front.

Drake pulled up on the end of the line and put the truck in park. Assessed their surroundings.

"Why do I have the impression we need to be armed to walk in here?"

"Trust me," Rink said. Pushed his door open. "That would not be a good idea."

Drake climbed out opposite him. Pocketed his keys and crunched across the frozen grass to the front door.

Rink paused for him to catch up and knocked twice. The door swung open as if by itself.

Rink glanced once at Drake and stepped inside.

A deep uneasiness settled into Drake's stomach as he followed.

CHAPTER TWENTY

Stale.

Air. Peanuts. Beer.

The combined smells hit Drake like a wall as he walked in. So pungent it brought a bit of moisture to his eyes.

Just as fast, he shook it off. Became acutely aware of the half-dozen men staring straight at them.

Side by side, he and Rink walked three steps into the room and stopped. Remained still. Swung their gaze in a full arc.

One end of the room served as a makeshift bar. A homemade counter constructed from plywood and two-by-fours. Stood about four feet tall, stretched almost from wall to wall.

Just enough room left open for the bartender with grizzled grey hair to slide past.

Seated at it were two men close in age and appearance. Early 30s. Hair grown out a bit further than Drake's. Suntanned.

Clearly not home more than a month or so themselves.

The opposite end of the place housed a pair of pool tables lined up square. The one on the left stood empty. On the right was a pair of men in their 40s. Jeans and flannels.

Both leaned against their cues. Stared.

The last man in the room was the oldest by at least a decade. Steel grey hair shorn into a flattop. Plaid shirt tucked into jeans. Hiking boots laced tight.

He sat with a newspaper before him and finished the article he was reading before looking up.

Every person in the room seemed to hold their breath as he did so.

He aimed his gaze at Rink. Shifted it to Drake. Ran it the length of him. Returned to Rink.

"This the guy?"

"It is," Rink said.

The man extended a hand to the remaining chairs around the table. "Have a seat."

The words snapped whatever spell the room was under. At once, the brothers at the bar returned to their beers. The men in the back resumed their game of pool.

There was no doubt, this was the old man's house.

Drake waited a moment for Rink to be seated. Remained standing and extended his hand to the man. "Drake Bell. Good to meet you."

The man looked at the hand, up at Drake. Paused a moment. Reached out and accepted the shake.

It felt like iron in Drake's grip.

"Jensen Hall."

Drake nodded. Settled himself down into his chair.

"The General here is who set up your meeting in Helena this morning," Rink added.

"Thank you for doing so," Drake said. "I appreciate it."

"Didn't do it for you," Hall replied. Not hostile. Deadpan. "I hope it helped."

"Insofar as it eliminated the prosecution's top angle, yes, very much so," Drake replied.

Hall leveled his gaze on Drake. "But?"

"But it brought me no closer to figuring out why he did it."

A small grunt from Hall. A curt nod of the head.

"And that is important?"

"Very," Drake said. "Establishes motive. Might be the key to the entire defense. May even keep there from needing to be a defense."

"Is there any way he didn't do it?" Hall asked. Narrowed his eyes.

Drake paused. Matched the stare. "No."

Hall held it another moment. Glanced over to Rink and nodded. "Good."

The word surprised Drake. He made no attempt to hide it.

"Good?"

"Not what you said," Hall clarified. "Just the fact that you said it. No offense, but we've all had our share of encounters with lawyers over the years."

A bit of understanding dawned on Drake. He glanced to Rink. "You wanted to see if I'd lie to you."

"I did," Hall said. No effort to obscure his intention. "You didn't, so now we can talk."

A dozen different comments came to Drake's mind. Some were questions. Some were confirmations. A few were smartass remarks.

He let all of them pass.

"You mind if I ask you a few questions?" Drake said.

"I assume that's why you're here," Hall said. "Go ahead."

Drake drew in a breath. Thought back to his notes still tucked in his bag in the truck.

Hoped he remembered everything he wanted to ask.

"Did you know Lukas Webb?"

"Not directly," Hall said. Shook his head. "I mean, I knew there was a sniper out there from Hamilton, but that's all."

"So he was well known?"

"No more than the next guy," Hall said. "But I made it my business to keep up on the local kids."

"Did you request them under your command?" Drake asked.

Hall shook his head again. "No. I wanted to have eyes in as many places as possible."

"Eyes for what?" Drake asked. Blurted the words out before he even thought to stop himself.

Again Hall leveled his gaze on Drake. "Is that important?"

The response was sharper than Drake expected. His lips parted a bit as he stared at the old man. After a few seconds, shook his head.

"No, it's not," Drake conceded. Paused a moment. Drew in a breath.

"This morning I spoke to Dr. Woodson. She said that Lukas was one of the most well-adjusted returning soldiers she'd ever encountered."

He let the statement linger. Hoped Hall might take the bait. Open up something he had not yet considered.

The General did not.

"I have not seen his military record, but the doctor and his sister both told me it was clean."

Again, Hall revealed nothing.

"Now, I know I've never met the man before, and I've only been looking into this a few days, but my immediate reaction is what happened had nothing to do with the military."

Drake glanced to Rink. Back to Hall.

"Am I correct in my thinking, or am I missing something?"

A moment passed as Hall continued to study him. "I have no doubt you're missing plenty, but I've had my own guys looking into things as well. So far, your conclusion is valid."

Drake chalked up a mental point in his favor.

"May I ask, how connected are you to the local community?"

The question drew a smirk.

Hall held his arms out by his side. Pointed to the Don't Tread On Me flag on one wall. At the closed circuit television above the bar that had watched Rink and Drake enter a short time before.

"As you can see, we pretty well keep to ourselves."

Drake passed his gaze over the items Hall pointed to. Noted a gun rack behind the bar.

The glances every other person gave them from time to time.

"So you're not aware of anything going on that might have caused his actions?"

"Like I said, nothing we've been able to find so far."

"Is there anybody around that might have reason to hide something?" Drake pressed.

"Not that I'm aware of," Hall said. "But again, we're digging."

"How about the man that shot Lukas?" Drake asked.

Hall's features hardened in response. The brothers at the bar both turned and glared.

For a moment, Drake feared he might have said the wrong thing.

He soon learned their venom was aimed not at him, but the person he was asking about.

"Hank McIlvaine is not a man," Hall said. Voice with a razor's edge. "He is a deserter. A disgrace to the uniform."

Drake's jaw dropped a half-inch. He glanced around the room.

"So, he doesn't..."

"No," Hall said. "That man knows better than to ever come here. This establishment is for honorable veterans only."

"He doesn't fit the bill."

Drake nodded. There was no need to press the matter further. He knew to look into Hank McIlvaine further.

That was enough on that front for the time being.

"Francis here mentioned you weren't charging the Webb's anything for your service," Hall said.

The statement seemed to come from nowhere. Drake wasn't sure if it was a question, but nodded anyway.

"That's right."

"Appreciate it," Hall said. "But if that becomes a problem, we can pay you. We take care of our own here."

"Shouldn't be a problem at all," Drake said. "I might have questions over the next couple weeks if you don't mind, but money isn't an issue."

Hall nodded. Said nothing.

Drake glanced to Rink, who met his gaze, flicked his eyes toward the door.

The statement from Hall wasn't out of the blue. It was a sign that the conversation was over.

Drake nodded in understanding. Stood.

"Mr. Hall, thank you for meeting with us," Drake said. Held out his hand again.

Hall stood as well. Shook it.

"You come back if you need anything else. Just remember, not many people know where to find us. I trust you'll keep this location to yourself."

"I will," Drake said. "You have my word."

The two men released grips. Drake and Rink headed for the door.

Drake got almost to it when a final question crossed his mind. He stopped and turned, his momentum still carrying him away.

"General Hall, let me ask you something. Is there any way a trained Army sniper opens fire on a public meeting and doesn't hit somebody?"

The old man looked at Drake and smiled.

"Only if it wasn't a somebody he was trying to hit."

CHAPTER TWENTY-ONE

393.

A 4-year-old heifer with a solid black hide. A single splotch of white near her hip.

Not once did she object as McIlvaine singled her out from the herd surrounding the barn and slipped a lead rope around her neck.

One large carrot was all it took to get her attention.

A second won her affection.

A few others smelled the carrot in the air as they walked by. Feigned interest for a moment. Just as fast lost it. Went back to huddling tight against one another.

The ground, churned up by dozens of hooves and frozen solid, passed uneven beneath McIlvaine's boots. More than once he cursed as he stumbled.

Tugged harder on the lead rope than intended.

Behind him, 393 picked her way over the rocky ground without incident. Focused all her attention on the carrot.

Chewed loudly.

Once the second carrot was gone, she slowed her pace. Pushed her enormous skull into McIlvaine's hip. Almost tossed him to the ground.

He gave up a third carrot without opposition.

It took 10 minutes for him to pull her around to the front of the barn. Away from the other animals, he slid a pair of pliers from his back pocket. Removed the tag from her ear.

Led her out through the gate.

On the other side of it sat his truck, a one-horse trailer hitched to it. The gate on it stood open, a metal ramp leading up into the back.

A small pile of apples sat in the middle of the floor. All sliced in half, aroma permeating the air.

Three-Nine-Three caught their scent the moment they passed through the gate. Tugged hard on the lead. Almost jerked McIlvaine from his feet.

This time, it drew a scowl. "I'm starting to feel a lot better about this."

From that point on, the heavy lifting was done by 393's stomach.

She walked a straight path to the trailer. Climbed aboard and started in on the apples.

McIlvaine closed the gate behind her. Circled around to the bed of his truck. Fished out the improvised brand he'd made a few weeks before.

A handheld blow torch.

The smell of acetylene filled his nostrils as it kicked to life. Shot out a blue-orange flame. Hissed in the darkness.

Holding it in one hand, he gripped the brand in the other. Passed the torch over it until the metal glowed red hot.

Returned back to the end of the trailer.

Inside, he could hear 393 chomping on the apples. Head down, her attention trained on the unexpected feast.

He kept the flame focused on the brand a moment longer. Slid it between the metal bars on the rear gate. Tossed the torch to the side.

For a brief second, the night was still. No sound at all but the rhythmic chewing of the tranquil beast as McIlvaine lined up the brand.

The silence ended with the searing sound of hot metal on rawhide.

The smell of burnt hair and flesh filled McIlvaine's nostrils. Brought a sheen of tears to his eyes.

Inside the rig, 393 forgot about the apples. Threw her head back. Bawled into the night.

The sound of her pained cries echoed out across the empty fields.

The entire trailer rocked under her weight as she bounced up and down. Alternated throwing her front and back end into the air.

McIlvaine extracted the brand and took a step back. Waved the scent away from his face. Watched as the heifer bucked herself tired.

Using the instep of his boot, he pushed some snow into a pile. Stuck the brand into the middle of it. Watched as steam rose from the hissing metal.

The pile melted into water.

Once it was cool, he tossed it and the torch back into the bed of his truck. Climbed into the cab. Pulled off his gloves. Took up his cellphone from the dash.

Tierney answered after a single ring.

"Yeah?" Voice low. Terse.

"She's loaded up," McIlvaine replied.

No need for further explanation. His call was expected.

"Good. Any problems?"

McIlvaine glanced into the rearview mirror. Could see 393's head return to the apples.

"None."

"Good," Tierney repeated. "You know where to take her?"

McIlvaine nodded in the darkness. "Same place as before, right?"

"Right."

"You sure that's the best idea?" McIlvaine asked.

"Why wouldn't it be?" Tierney snapped. Voice still low. Now a trace of hostility present. "Where else would we take her? The damn thing is branded, remember?"

McIlvaine shook his head. Glared back at his reflection in the rearview mirror.

"You're right. I'm on my way now."

The call ended without another word.

Muttering to himself, McIlvaine put the truck in gear. Drove away into the darkness.

CHAPTER TWENTY-TWO

Wednesday morning.

Most weeks, a time reserved for Zoo Crew outings.

Given the holidays and Ajax's absence, it was decided to hold off until Friday.

Two things stood out to Drake as he woke and stared up at the ceiling in the early morning half-light.

First was the simple fact that he wasn't jumping up to head off somewhere. After the same three-a-week routine for seven years, his body was accustomed to getting moving.

Missing Monday for Christmas Day was a pleasant respite.

Missing two consecutive outings left him restless.

The second was how quiet the house became without Ajax around. No late night video gaming. No food deliveries showing up at odd hours. No sound of feet shuffling back and forth to the kitchen.

Instead, all he had was the steady snoring of Suzy Q pressed against his leg. Burrowed down into the covers, wrinkled face smashed down so tight he couldn't discern her eyes or mouth from the other folds of skin.

Drake rolled over and checked the clock. Square red digits stared back at him. Told him it was just after 7:00. Still almost an hour before Kade arrived.

He did a quick check in his head of his options.

The gym on campus was closed for the winter break and it was too cold to run outside.

That left only a bodyweight workout in the living room. Something he hated doing. Only resorted to in the direst of situations.

If he had any hope of clearing his head though, of unraveling what happened before Lukas woke from his coma, he had to burn off some excess energy.

Starting at his closet, he layered up as if going outside. Thermal pants. Wool socks. Polypropylene long sleeve shirt. Fleece pullover atop it. Knit cap. Gloves.

Suzy Q grunted her disapproval as he went into the living room. Started with a few hundred jumping jacks. Went straight into body weight squats. Pushups. Sit-ups. Mountain climbers.

When he was done with the circuit, he made another pass through.

Then another.

By the time he was finished, sweat dripped from the tip of his nose. Ran the length of his face.

His clothing stuck to his body.

Moving fast, he dumped the wet garments in the laundry basket. Showered. Dressed.

Forced Q outside to do her business and filled her bowls in the kitchen.

Stepped out onto the front walk at two minutes before 8:00 to find Kade climbing from his truck parked along the curb.

"Are my eyes deceiving me?" Drake asked. Faux surprise in his voice. "When I told you 8:00, I didn't think there was a chance I'd see you before noon."

Kade smirked at the comment. Waved with one finger at him.

"I'll have you know that I was home and in bed by 10:00 last night. Sage can vouch for me."

Drake raised his eyebrows in disbelief. Headed for his truck. "Strike out at Blue's again?"

"Hell no. You know I've got a perfect record in that joint. It's even written on the bathroom wall. They talk about it in hushed whispers," Kade said. Circled around to the passenger side.

"I thought that was because of something you caught in the bath-room?" Drake said. Started the truck and turned the heater fan down low as cold air piped in.

"Cute," Kade said. Pursed his lips in mock indignation.

"It was either they were closed or your mama stuffed you so full last night before leaving you barely made it back before falling asleep," Drake said. "So which is it?"

Kade kept the look in place. Stared out the window. "The latter. Where we headed this morning anyway?"

A knowing grin crossed Drake's face. Forced his head up and down in a small nod.

Still, he let it go without comment.

"Back to Hamilton. I wanted to check out the hall where they were having the Agriculture Commission meeting."

Kade held his hands out over the vents. Felt warm air. Turned the fan up higher.

"And what are you hoping to find there?"

"No idea," Drake confessed.

"Awesome," Kade said. "And you wanted me to come along at the crack of dawn because...?"

"Because if you're going to be an investigator, you need to get used to doing this sort of thing."

"Hey, I haven't agreed to that yet," Kade countered.

"No," Drake conceded, "but you haven't said no either."

The topic of conversation shifted to the upcoming NFL playoffs as Drake angled them south through the Bitterroot Valley. The sun was a bit late rising, announcing its arrival with authority.

Light danced off the Bitterroot River to their left. Refracted off errant patches of snow to the right.

Caused them both to lower their visors in front of them.

Ten minutes shy of 9:00, Drake parked the truck outside the Town Hall.

A one-story structure, the building stretched 30' across. Twice that in length.

The entire outside was done in red brick. No windows. A pair of double glass doors out front.

No signs of life anywhere.

"Looks like nobody's home," Kade commented.

"Only one way to find out," Drake replied. Pushed open his door to be greeted by a puff of icy wind.

Opposite him, Kade did the same. Sucked in a deep breath as the air passed over his body.

Gravel crunched beneath their feet as they walked toward the front door. Said nothing.

Drake was the first to reach it. Extracted a hand from his pocket. Grasped the frigid metal handle.

It pulled open without a bit of resistance. Warm air gushed out to greet them.

Holding the door open behind him, Drake stepped through. Stood in the buffer zone between the doors a moment. Let the overhead fans blow heat down on them.

Pressed through the second door and into the town hall.

Side by side, they stood in a narrow hallway extending in either direction. Polished hardwood floor underfoot.

A pair of double doors standing open in front of them. Sagging crime scene tape draped across the opening.

"We are allowed to be here, right?" Kade asked.

"Well, it's not like I asked anybody," Drake asked. Ducked beneath the tape. Stepped into the main room.

"That's my boy," Kade replied. Followed right behind.

The smell of gunpowder and sulfur still hung in the air.

It appeared nothing had been touched since the incident five days before. Chairs were scattered, pushed to the side. A table at the front of the room was turned on edge.

Sunlight filtered through frosted glass. Gave the room a ghostly pallor.

"Kind of spooky, huh?" Drake whispered.

Earned himself a snort in response.

"You white boys are all the same," Kade said. Walked forward. Started scanning the floor for clues.

The movement sparked Drake from his trance. Drew out a chuckle. "You realize your father is whiter than I am, right?"

"Maybe, but my mom's not," Kade said.

Drake shook his head in mirth. Bent at the waist. Drew up a piece of paper from the floor.

"Anything good?" Kade asked.

"Agenda for the meeting," Drake said. Scanned the list. Didn't recognize any of the items on it.

Extended the paper to Kade. "You familiar with any of this stuff?"

Kade cocked his head. Looked at it without taking it.

"Naw, but ranching isn't really my thing. Hang onto it, though. Has to be somebody around that can translate."

Drake nodded. Pocketed the paper. Moved to the front of the room. Examined the table and chairs lying on their side.

Walked past them to the back wall. Looked at the rows of pictures hanging in order.

Top tier, City Counsel.

Second level, County Commission.

One below it, Agriculture Commission.

Kade stepped beside Drake and scanned the photos. Found the exact same thing his friend was staring at.

"Yesterday, Rink set up a meeting for me with a group of veterans out in the woods south of here," Drake said. Jutted his chin toward the wall. "The last thing I asked them before I left was if there was any way a trained Army sniper opened fire in here and didn't hit anybody."

Kade paused a moment. Waited to see if Drake would continue.

He did not.

"What did they say?" Kade asked.

"They laughed. Told me maybe it wasn't a somebody he was trying to hit."

Kade snorted. Nodded. Stared at the pair of bullet holes that took out both eyes in the picture of Holt Tierney.

"I'd say they were right."

"You ever heard of this guy?" Drake asked.

Kade shook his head. "Never. You?"

"Nope. What say we go pay him a visit?"

CHAPTER TWENTY-THREE

Speed dial three.

Number one was Bernice. Always had been. Rarely got used.

The second was Rex Johnson. Was called into action a minimum twice a week. Usually more. Sometimes much more.

Third in the pecking order was McIlvaine. Added less than a month before. Used only a couple of times.

This was one such time.

The line rang twice before McIlvaine's voice responded. Sounded a little groggy. A bit irritated.

"Yeah?"

Holt ignored the insubordination. Launched right into his reason for calling.

"I've got someone here to see me. I'm going to leave you on speaker-phone. I want you to listen in."

"Who is it?"

The sound of McIlvaine moving around could be heard over the line.

"Drake Bell," Holt said. Checked the name he'd jotted down just a moment before to be sure.

The movement on the other end stopped. "Who the hell is Drake Bell?"

Holt pushed out a sigh. Rolled his eyes. "Lukas Webb's attorney."

"Oh, shit," McIlvaine said. Started moving again. "When?"

"Right now, you idiot," Holt spat. "They just stopped by the office and asked if I had a few minutes. I told the secretary to give me two minutes and send them in."

It sounded like McIlvaine snorted, spat, on the other end. "Alright, go ahead."

Holt muted the cellphone. Tucked it up against a stack of papers on his desk, out of sight. Pretended to be looking at his computer as the door opened.

Through it walked two young men in their mid-20s, both well built. One a little taller, little thicker. Blonde hair shorn short.

The other looked part Native American. An ethnic mixture of some sort. Long dark hair.

Holt stood as they entered. Extended his hand across the desk and introduced himself.

The blonde took the lead.

"Thank you for seeing us, Mr. Tierney. My name is Drake Bell, this is my investigator Kade Keuhl. We've been retained by the family of Lukas Webb to look into the shooting last weekend."

All three settled down into seats.

Holt put on a grave expression. Shook his head. Bit back the twinge of anxiety that passed through him.

"Looking into it?"

"Well, as you know, Mr. Webb is being kept in a coma," Drake said. "So nobody is really sure why he did what he did. Given that the Sheriff has a guard posted by his door waiting for him to wake so he can haul him off to jail, we're looking into things now."

Holt nodded. "Yes, I saw on the news the other night that Paula Goslin is talking about asking for the maximum sentence against him. Such an ugly situation."

"Very," Drake said. Glanced over to Kade. "Do you mind if we ask you a few questions?"

"By all means," Holt said. Leaned back. Raised his eyebrows. "I don't know a lot, but you're welcome to it."

Drake nodded. "Appreciate it. I understand you serve on the Agriculture Commission, correct?"

"I do," Holt said. "Have for almost 30 years."

"And that you're now the Chair?" Drake asked.

"Co-chair," Holt corrected. "Myself and Wanda Pritchett."

Drake jotted the name down. "Can I ask, what exactly does the Commission do?"

The feeling of uneasiness began to recede within Holt. They weren't sniffing around him with any suspicion.

They were merely gathering baseline information.

He laced his fingers behind his head and leaned back further in his chair.

"In short, it depends. Our chief concern is to be a pass-through for information from the state to the producers. If new laws are enacted, new zoning regulations, vaccination requirements, that sort of thing."

Again Drake wrote down the information. Flicked his gaze over to Kade. "Doesn't seem like the kind of thing to get a rifle and start shooting over."

Holt shook his head in earnest. "No, it doesn't. I think the sheer shock value of it has hit us all harder than the act itself."

"Really?" Kade asked. Let the surprise show in his voice.

"Of course," Holt answered. "This is Montana. We've all been around a rifle being fired before. But indoors? Over something so innocuous?"

Drake and Kade both nodded in assent.

"Have you, or any of the other commissioners, had any trouble with Lukas Webb in the past?" Drake asked.

"Never," Holt said. Tried out his best modest voice. "To be honest, I don't think we've even spoken in the last 15 years. Not since he was a boy and used to tag along with his father."

"Did you know Mr. Webb?" Kade asked.

"Every rancher in the area knows each other," Holt said.

"Were you close?" Drake asked.

"I'm not sure how you mean," Holt said. "Mitch Webb wasn't what you would call *close* with anybody. A small-time guy trying to make ends meet."

"So he might have had some animosity toward larger producers like yourself?" Kade asked.

A bit of a fire flashed behind Holt's eyes. He paused to make sure it was gone before pushing forward.

"Not at all. He was just always busy. In a hurry. Kept to himself. Far as I know though, he never had any trouble with anyone.

"As for myself, I was sad to hear he passed. We didn't even know he was sick, that's how much he kept his distance."

Drake nodded. Made another note.

"Can you tell us about the shooting itself?

Holt exhaled, glad to be moving on.

"We were going through some routine business when Lukas kept trying to raise his hand to speak. I was presiding over the meeting and explained to him that's not how things were done."

"Not how things were done?" Drake asked.

"You see, we abide by basic parliamentary procedure," Holt said. "We have a set agenda that the commission discusses. At the end, we open the floor for public comment.

"He was trying to skip all that. Demanded to be heard right that instant."

More notes taken.

"So you dismissed him?" Drake asked.

"Not at all," Holt replied. "I just told him he would have to wait until the public comment period to be heard. He didn't seem to like that, stormed off."

"So he was angry when he left?" Kade asked.

"Very," Holt said. "Fighting mad, or I guess as it were, shooting mad. Just jumped up and left."

"And then what happened?" Drake asked.

"We all thought that was the end of it," Holt said. "Went about the meeting until he walked back in and opened fire."

Drake took some more notes.

"I understand it was an employee of yours, a Hank McIlvaine, that put down Mr. Webb?"

"Yes, that's right," Holt said. "He's a consultant I hired a while back to help me streamline some things here at the ranch. I asked him to sit in on the meeting and see if there was anything that caught his ear we might do differently."

"So his being there wasn't as a security presence of any kind?" Kade asked.

"Certainly not," Holt said. "I knew about his military background, but I didn't know he carried a weapon."

Drake made a few more notes. Nodded. Looked up at Holt.

"Just lucky he was there, huh?"

Something about the question, the tone, caught Holt. The modesty fled from his features. Face hardened.

"I guess so." He stood. "Now, I am sorry to cut this short, but if you gentlemen will excuse me, I have a meeting with my ranch supervisor to get to."

Drake and Kade both stood. Shook hands again.

"Absolutely," Drake said. "Thank you for meeting with us."

Holt nodded. Walked them to the door. Watched out the window as they headed for their truck.

"Well, what did you make of that?" Holt asked aloud.

"You're good at what you do," McIlvaine said through the speakerphone. "I'll give you that."

"Managing people?" Holt asked.

"Lying out your ass."

CHAPTER TWENTY-FOUR

Wednesday.

The busiest night of the week on Drake's calendar.

A standing dinner date stretching back two years and counting.

It started not long after Sage first moved to Missoula. As low woman on the totem pole at St. Michael's Hospital, she was given the second shift.

Decided to stay there so her mornings were free to run with the Zoo Crew.

Not that she'd ever once admitted it.

In an effort to try and mitigate the damage to her social life, Drake started meeting her for dinner on Wednesdays.

Every Wednesday.

Sometimes he brought Kade or Ajax. Every once in a while he brought Q.

On occasion, he would bring food with him. Others, they would eat whatever the cafeteria was serving.

This week, Drake arrived solo and empty handed. Found Sage waiting for him by the door. Greeted her with a hug.

"No special delivery this week?" Sage asked. Feigned a pouting face.

"Sorry," Drake said. Spread his hands wide. "This week you just get me."

"Damn."

"Hey, blame your mama," Drake said. Held open the door to the cafeteria for her. "I don't think I've eaten since I left your house."

A knowing laugh slid from Sage as she passed through the door. "You don't know the half of it. You should see the mountain of food she sent home with Kade last night."

"I bet," Drake said. Followed her into the serving line. Took up a clear plastic plate. Piled it high with veggies.

"Please tell me that's not actually what you're eating for dinner," Sage said. Let disapproval and contempt drip from her tone.

Without glancing her way, Drake spread shredded cheese over the plate. Two scoops of bacon bits. Croutons. A hefty dollop of ranch dressing.

"Better?"

"Getting there," Sage said. Smirked. Fixed her own plate to match his.

Drake paid for their meals. Handed a bottle of water to Sage. Took up a sweet tea for himself.

Followed her to their preferred perch in the back corner.

"So tell me, what had you two out and about so early this morning?" Sage said. "Thanks for the invite, by the way."

"Wasn't your area of expertise," Drake said. "Besides, if I'm going to convince Kade to pursue becoming a PI for me, I need to get him involved."

Sage shoveled greens into her mouth. Looked at him in silence.

Finally conceded the point with a shrug.

"What were you guys up to anyway?" Sage asked. "I talked to Kade for a second earlier, he was damn near spitting mad."

"I'm aware," Drake deadpanned. "You should have been in the truck with him. I used to think having Ava ride shotgun was bad."

The comment stopped Sage's fork halfway to her mouth. She lowered it back to her plate. Arched an eyebrow.

"Oh yeah? And how is the lovely Ava?"

Drake smirked and shook his head. Let Sage know how ridiculous he thought the question was.

"She's good, thank you for asking. Wished us - *all* of us - a Merry Christmas just two days ago."

"I'm sure she did," Sage said. Returned to eating.

"And we all returned the sentiment," Drake said. Kept his face aimed downward to hide his smile.

"So, Kade was pissed earlier," Sage said. Blatant change of subject. No effort to hide it.

The smile on Drake's face grew wider. He looked up and shook his head again.

"We went down to Hamilton to take a look at the Town Hall where the shooting took place. Went over afterwards to meet with a guy named Holt Tierney."

"The rancher?" Sage asked.

Drake's fork stopped by his mouth. His eyes leveled on Sage.

"You know him?"

"Not *know him* know him. He was in the paper today," Sage said. Took a long pull from her bottle of water. "Big article about the shooting. How it shook everybody up, but he's still planning to host his annual Winter Ball on Friday as a sign that things are getting back to normal."

Drake dropped his fork. Leaned back. Looped an arm over the chair beside him. "Huh. I'll have to take a look at that."

"Too bad *Ava* isn't here to go with you," Sage added. Returned to eating without matching Drake's gaze.

"Cute," Drake replied. Continued to stare off at the wall. Thought about his earlier encounter with Tierney.

"So, again, spitting mad part?"

Without shifting his focus, Drake replied, "Old man lied through his teeth to us."

"Still..."

"And he was condescending as hell," Drake finished. Shifted his focus back to the table.

"That explains it," Sage said.

Drake nodded in agreement.

"Where is Kade tonight, anyway?" Sage asked.

"I think after a few days at home, he was itching to get back out on the prowl," Drake said.

"With my brother, the itching usually comes after the prowl," Sage said.

The retort drew a crooked smile from Drake. "Touché. Can't blame the guy right now, though. I think he's hopeful the holidays have pulled in a bit of fresh meat."

Sage coughed back a laugh.

"Ajax?"

Drake shook his head. "Not until Sunday."

"Ouch," Sage said. "So what's next for Sherlock Holmes and his horny sidekick?"

Drake ignored the joke. Chewed the last of his salad.

He'd been working on that very question since leaving Hamilton.

"Think out loud," Sage prompted.

Drake shifted his attention to Sage and shook his head. "I need to track down this Wanda Pritchett, the Co-Chair. So far the only version of events we've heard came from Tierney."

"A less-than-reliable source?"

"Sure seems that way," Drake said. "I have no idea why he's lying, but he seems hellbent on doing so."

"Okay," Sage said. "And then what?"

"I don't know," Drake admitted. "Depends what she has to say. Might go talk to the veterans group again. May head back to Memorial and pick Sara's brain some more."

Sage leaned back in her chair. Smiled.

Drake noticed the look. Rolled his eyes. "Don't. Sara is a client. And I'm not convinced Rink and her don't have a thing going."

"That's not what I was smiling about," Sage said. Held her hands up by her sides.

"Then what?"

"You're getting better at this. Remember that fiasco with the babies? You were like a bull in a China shop. Now, you're starting to let things come to you a little more."

Again Drake raised his eyebrows. Looked over the thinning dining room.

"Yeah, that was sloppy as hell," Drake admitted. "But I knew it. I just didn't see any other way."

"And now you do," Sage said. "That's all I'm saying."

Drake looked back at her. Nodded.

Said nothing.

CHAPTER TWENTY-FIVE

Gone With the Wind.

That was the first thing Drake thought as he parked the truck. Looked up at the enormous ranch house before him.

Two stories tall. Sweeping front porch. Thick white columns. Large trees dotting the front lawn.

"Damn," Drake muttered. Turned the engine off.

This wasn't a Montana cattle ranch. It was a southern cotton plantation.

On steroids.

Drake stepped out of the truck and walked toward the front door. Kade had offered to join him again, but he balked. Wasn't sure how long he would be. Where he was going after meeting with Wanda.

How she would take having two young men show up on your doorstep.

Outside, the day was a carbon copy of the one before. And the dozen before that.

Milky white sky. One unending cloud that blanketed the western half of the state. Threatened to unleash snow at any point.

Blustery, cold air. The smell of pine and ice crystals in the air.

His shoes clinked against the hardwood porch as he approached. Pressed the doorbell. Heard chimes playing throughout the house.

Several moments passed as he stood waiting. Picked up the sound of footsteps approaching.

The door swung open to reveal a woman somewhere between late-50s and early-70s. So little of her original self remained though, it made pinpointing an age difficult.

Lips a bit too full. Skin a touch too tight. Makeup applied with a heavy hand. Hair that was an unnatural shade of auburn-orange.

She gave Drake a onceover. Smiled and stepped to the side.

"Mr. Bell, please, come in."

"Thank you," Drake said. Stepped inside and wiped his feet. "I appreciate you meeting with me, Ms. Pritchett."

"Please, Wanda," she said. Waved a hand at him. Led him into a parlor to the right.

Drake followed her into the room and took a seat in an armchair. Everything in the room looked to fit with the southern plantation motif.

Bookshelves lined with leather-bound volumes. Furniture in red and gold designs. A baby grand piano.

"Can I get you anything?" Wanda asked. Settled herself down on the end of the couch across from him.

"Oh, no thank you," Drake said. "You have a beautiful home here."

Allowed his gaze to take it all in.

Again, Wanda waved at him. "I know it's a bit much, but my husband was from Georgia. Used to imagine himself as a Southern plantation owner.

"Gentleman Jay, that's what he used to jokingly refer to himself as."

Drake smiled. Nodded.

"I understand completely. I myself come from Tennessee.

Wanda smiled. Slapped her leg. "Oh, so you know exactly what I'm talking about."

"I do," Drake confirmed. "I know you must be quite busy, so I promise to keep this short."

"Nonsense," Wanda said. "Since Jay passed on, there isn't much for me to do around here."

"Oh," Drake said. Cursed himself for not picking up on her use of the past tense when first speaking about her husband. "I had no idea."

Again, careful not to dole out false apologies.

"That's how I came to be on the Commission to begin with," Wanda said. "When he passed two years ago, I stepped in to finish his term."

"I see," Drake said. "And the ranch here, do you still...?"

"Oh yes," Wanda said. "Every bit as many cattle as we were working when Jay was still around. He was always very meticulous about running the place like a business. Wanted to make sure it would keep on going long after he and I were gone."

"Wow," Drake said. "Very impressive."

There were no false congratulations in the statement. He truly meant it.

"I understand you're working for Lukas Webb?" Wanda asked.

"The family has asked me to look into the incident, yes," Drake said. Didn't want to use the word *shooting*.

The answer wasn't entirely the truth. Wasn't entirely a lie either.

He decided to leave it at that.

"You were there that night, right?" Drake asked.

"I was," Wanda said. "So terrible. So very terrible."

She shifted her focus toward the window. Watched as a car rolled by on the road outside. Waited until it was gone before continuing.

"Holt and I are co-chairs, so we were seated in the middle of the table. Frank and Harvey sit on the left. Billy beside me on the right."

Her gaze went back to Drake. "All a bunch of ranchers here in the valley for decades. Major boy's network. The only reason I'm there is because of what happened to Jay."

Drake nodded. Boy's networks in Montana were something he was beginning to understand.

Fast.

"If you don't mind," Drake said. Kept his voice low and even. Not quite soothing or patronizing. "Can you walk me through it?"

Wanda pushed out a heavy sigh. Dropped her shoulders several inches with the exertion.

"There isn't a whole lot to tell. We were on the second item of our agenda when Lukas raised his hand to speak. Holt turned him down and told him he had to wait until public comment.

"Lukas didn't much care for that and tried to speak anyway. Holt got a little red, threatened to have him removed, so Lukas got up and left."

Several questions sprang to mind, but Drake let them pass. Didn't want to interrupt her rhythm. Wanted the entire story out before he started pecking at individual aspects.

"I thought the whole thing was a little unnecessary, but didn't think much else about it," Wanda continued.

"A few minutes passed and we moved on to the next topic. Harvey was the point person on it, so I was looking down the table at him when the first shot went off. Sounded like a thunderclap inside the room.

"And the light, oh my, the light. You've never seen such a thing. After that, one of the men flipped the table up on its edge and we ducked down behind it. We heard a second rifle shot, then a bunch of smaller shots fired.

"After, we just kind of huddled where we were for a while. Waited for all that light to fade away. Once we emerged from behind the table, most of the people in the room had cleared out.

"I could hear sirens in the distance."

By the time the last sentence came out, Wanda's voice was just above a whisper. Her hands were folded in her lap, fingers twisted together.

A bit of moisture lined her eyes.

"What happened after that?" Drake asked. His voice low to match hers.

Wanda made no attempt to look at him as she answered. Her voice and her gaze both had a distant quality to them.

"The police were the first to show. They secured the scene. Right after that came the paramedics. They determined Lukas was still alive, loaded him up and took him away.

"How he survived all those shots we heard, I don't know."

Drake nodded. "You mentioned that the whole thing felt a bit unnecessary. What did you mean by that?"

The puff of auburn-orange hair remained in place as Wanda shook her head from side to side.

"In my time on the board, we've never been what you would call sticklers for procedure. Most of the time, if somebody wished to speak, they spoke."

"Any idea why Mr. Tierney made such a show of wanting Lukas to wait for the public comment period?" Drake asked.

The fingers continued to writhe in her lap. "Public comment was something he put in place a couple meetings back. Said it would make us more efficient.

"Most of the time our meetings are pretty simple, so there was no call for comments of any kind."

Drake grunted. The actions Wanda was describing and the placement of Lukas's shots were beginning to link up.

Their significance was not quite clear to Drake.

That would be next on his to-do list.

"Do you remember what it was that Lukas wanted to speak on?" Drake asked.

Wanda nodded. "We were discussing the new state designation plan."

The words held no meaning at all to Drake. He had seen them on the agenda he picked up from the crime scene.

Nothing else came to mind.

"State designation plan?" Drake asked.

Wanda nodded. Remained with her gaze aimed out the window. "It has to do with how the state handles brucellosis. I'll be honest, I don't know a lot about it. The company runs the ranch now, I just sign things when they bring them to me."

"That's quite alright," Drake said. "I'm more interested in what happened that night right now."

Wanda nodded.

"Just one more question and then I'll be on my way," Drake said. "I can tell this is difficult for you to relive."

Another nod.

"What did you mean by *the light*?"

Wanda blinked twice. Turned her head at the neck to face him.

"It was nothing I've ever seen before. Bright red light that hung in the air. Like standing next to a flare, or a firework, or something."

CHAPTER TWENTY-SIX

Boredom.

Much worse than sitting through an Agriculture Commission meeting.

Having to sit and do surveillance.

McIlvaine slid his body low behind the wheel. Rubbed his fingers together in front of him. Blew on them in an attempt at warmth.

Didn't dare turn on the engine. Didn't want the sound to be heard or the exhaust to be seen rising in the air.

A flash of movement drew his attention to the front door of the house. Caused him to slide a little lower in his seat.

The guy Holt had told him to follow - Drake Bell - emerged. The old lady with a bad dye job from the meeting followed him out.

They stood and talked for a moment on the porch. The old hag even gave him a hug before the guy climbed into his truck and drove away.

McIlvaine waited a full minute before starting his own rig. Pulled out of the tree-lined lane he was parked in just down the road.

Laying on the gas, he followed the single road back into town. Took the curves fast. Caught sight of the black truck ahead of him within two miles.

Easing his foot off the accelerator, McIlvaine followed the remaining five miles back into town. Used the cover of traffic to pull a little closer.

Figured out within three blocks where they were headed.

Stayed close behind Bell to make sure.

Fifteen minutes after leaving the Pritchett Ranch, the black truck pulled into Hamilton Memorial Hospital.

"Shit," McIlvaine muttered. Drove on past. Went a quarter mile down the road and turned into the parking lot of a Catholic Church.

He turned the truck around so he was facing out toward the hospital. Took up his cellphone and hit send.

It was answered after a single ring.

"Tierney."

Same indifferent voice. Same undercurrent of condescension.

McIlvaine felt the muscles in his jaw contract. Shook his head to the side.

"Yeah, it's me."

"Find out anything?"

"The kid met with Pritchett. From there, he came straight back to the hospital. He's inside now."

The information was met with a moment of silence. McIlvaine waited it out.

The old man loved giving orders. He'd spit them out again soon enough if there was something he wanted done.

He always did.

"How long was he in there?" Tierney asked.

McIlvaine checked the clock on the dash. Worked the math backwards in his head.

"Twenty minutes. Twenty-five at most."

"Hmm," Tierney grunted. Again fell to silence.

Once more, McIlvaine waited him out.

"Where are you now?"

McIlvaine twisted in his seat. Glanced over at the sign along the front of the church. A simple affair, white letters against a brown backdrop.

"The Catholic Church of Hamilton parking lot. He turned into the hospital, I went on so as to not draw suspicion."

Another few moments of silence. The sound of chewing over the line.

"Alright, stay put a while longer," Tierney said. "See how long he stays at the hospital, where he heads after he leaves."

A derisive snort slid out from McIlvaine. "How long is a while longer?"

"Long enough to see if he heads north toward Missoula or goes somewhere else."

"And if he does?"

"Stay on him."

CHAPTER TWENTY-SEVEN

Obvious.

Blatantly, impossible-to-ignore, almost an insult, obvious.

That's how glaringly out of place the tail was.

Drake spotted the truck the moment he pulled away from the Pritchett Ranch. Just a couple hundred yards away from the house, parked in tight beside a clump of trees.

Dark silhouette sitting low behind the wheel.

Every bit of land on both sides of the road was owned by the Pritchett's. There were no other houses in either direction.

No reason for the truck to be there.

Drake pretended not to notice and drove on toward town. Alternated his gaze between the front windshield and the rearview mirror.

Saw the truck come into sight a few miles outside of town. Slow its pace. Remain a constant distance back from him.

Once he reached the edge of Hamilton he took out his cellphone. Scrolled through his call log. Hit Send.

Rink answered after three rings. Sound of skates and sticks audible behind him.

"Yes, sir," Rink said. Sounds behind him faded away.

"Hey, where are you at right now?" Drake asked.

"Practice," Rink said. "Why? What's going on, should I head down?"

Rink, a former hockey standout that accounted for the nickname everybody knew him by, now coached the Missoula Marauders hockey team. Somewhere between college and the NHL in terms of talent.

Light years from either on the grounds of prestige.

"I've got a tail," Drake said. "Headed toward the hospital now."

"Shit," Rink muttered.

"I was going to ask you to trade rigs with me for a while."

"Like I said, I can leave now," Rink said. "Or, Sara is there. You want me to call her?"

Drake weighed the information a moment. Eased through a yellow light. Changed into the outer lane as he crossed into town.

"Yeah, please. Ask her to move her car around back. I'll park out front and go in. Find a side entrance and take her ride from there. Won't be but an hour or so."

"Done," Rink said. Signed off without another word.

Drake flipped the phone onto the seat beside him. Checked his rearview mirror.

Spotted the truck matching his movements a block back.

Slowing his pace, he turned into the Hamilton Memorial Hospital parking lot. Drove along the back of it, keeping his truck parallel to the road.

Waited for his tail to catch up.

Just as the two trucks pulled even, nothing more than a sidewalk and a patch of grass separating them, Drake chanced a glance over.

Felt a flash of recognition in the back of his mind.

It was replaced immediately by a flush of anger.

Turning the truck toward the hospital, he parked and went inside. Found Sara waiting for him outside the cafeteria. Forced himself to swallow down the venom inside before speaking.

This wasn't her fault.

"Is your car around back?" Drake asked. No salutation of any kind. Hints of tension in his voice.

"It is," Sara said. Noticed both. Wrapped her arms across himself. "What's going on?"

"I'm being followed," Drake said. "I need to go out and talk to the

Home Guard again real quick, but damned sure can't go with someone watching me."

Sara nodded.

"I'll explain everything when I return," Drake said. Pulled some of the vitriol from his voice. Tried to sound reassuring. "I just need a couple answers before I do."

"I understand," Sara said. Extended her keys toward him. Four brass implements held together by a simple ring. "I'll be here when you get back."

"Thank you," Drake said. Accepted the keys. "What I am looking for out there?"

"Ford Ranger," Sara said. "Faded red, little bit of rust. It's a farm truck, you'll know it when you see it."

Drake nodded and headed toward a side entrance.

For the first time in months, he didn't notice the cold as he stepped outside. In fact, he felt warmth creeping up along his back. Pushed his sleeves up, scanned the lot.

Just as Sara said, the Ranger jumped out at him, obvious in the side lot. Most of the cars there were BMW's and Audi's, no doubt the preferred parking for the doctors on staff.

If not for the torrent of emotions roiling through him, Drake might have even laughed at the truck sitting front and center.

The proverbial ugly puppy in the pet shop window begging to be picked.

Drake found the doors unlocked and climbed in. Started the truck and swung out the back entrance. Took three side streets before turning up through the middle of town.

Watched his mirrors the entire time.

No sign of the tail behind him.

His breath slowed a bit as he pushed on. Followed the same path he and Rink had taken just a couple days before.

The cluster of cars at the cabin was a bit bigger than his previous trip. The same four trucks were parked in the exact spots as before.

Beside them was an aging Firebird and a muddy Jeep.

Drake pulled up on the far edge and stepped out. Willed himself to move slow. To make sure his hands were visible at all times.

A fresh dusting of snow stuck to his shoes as he walked for the front door. Knocked twice. Had it swing open for him once again.

Drake stepped inside. Stopped and waited.

The crowd had grown to keep pace with the cars outside. A new pair of men was working the second pool table. Early 30s. Close-cropped hair. Patchy beards.

One nearly a foot taller than the other.

At the sight of him, the pair of brothers at the bar turned back to their drinks. The bartender went back to wiping down glasses.

In the center of the room, Jensen Hall looked up from a paperback. One corner of his mouth played up in a smile.

"Mr. Bell. I wondered if we might be seeing you again."

Drake took it as an invitation. Walked over and seated himself across from Hall.

"I'm very sorry to barge in like this."

The smile spread across Hall's entire face. He pointed to the closed circuit television behind the bar.

"Nobody gets within 100 feet of this place unless we say so. We didn't recognize the truck at first, but you did the right thing approaching like you did."

Drake nodded. "It's Sara Webb's. I had to trade her a little bit ago."

"Everything alright?"

"I'm being followed," Drake said. Hoped it would have the intended effect he was going for.

It did.

The smile faded from Hall's face.

"Followed? By whom?"

"I only got a quick glimpse of him," Drake said. "But I'm 80% sure it was Hank McIlvaine."

At the mention of the name, the brothers turned from the bar. Drake saw them from the corner of his eye. Stone expressions on both their faces.

"You're sure?" Hall asked. Narrowed his eyes a bit.

"Like I said, 80%. Just started today, as I was leaving the Pritchett Ranch. Followed me clear in town to the hospital."

"We can take care of that," Hall said. No hesitation at all in his voice. No hint of concern.

"I appreciate that," Drake said. "And might take you up on that soon enough, but right now I don't think he knows I'm on to him. I'd rather keep it that way, at least a little longer."

"Don't worry," Hall said. "He won't know we're on to him either."

Drake considered the words. Knew better than to argue.

Nodded in appreciation.

"I have two questions for you," Drake said.

Hall motioned forward with his hand for them.

"The first is, who is Hank McIlvaine? You mentioned the other day you don't associate with him, but I saw a news report the other night claiming he was a veteran."

For the first time, Drake noticed that sounds of pool had faded away. He flicked his gaze to the corner. Noticed all four men leaning on their cues.

Listening close.

"He is not one of us, if that's what you're asking," Hall said. Bitterness obvious in his voice. "Saying Hank McIlvaine was in the military is like saying the guy who sweeps Wrigley Field is a Cub. He was in for about two months before developing some mysterious ailment and taking a medical discharge."

"Any idea what he does now?" Drake asked.

"Besides suckling benefits and giving veterans everywhere a bad name? Low-level guerilla for hire. Nothing more."

Drake nodded. "Should I be worried?"

"No," Hall said. "We were going to take care of McIlvaine anyway for what he did to Lukas. This just accelerates our timetable a little bit."

The news blew Drake back a bit. Raised his eyebrows up his forehead.

"If it's all the same to you, I'm going to pretend I didn't hear that."

"Good boy," Hall said. Bowed his head.

Whether it was appreciation or acknowledgment, Drake wasn't sure.

"Alright, second question," Drake said. "Can a flare be fired from a rifle?"

Confusion clouded Hall's face. He said nothing.

Drake paused. Considered how to better ask the question.

"Wanda Pritchett mentioned several times that once Lukas fired his first shot, there was a blinding red light in the room. Talked about it a half-dozen times. Said it blocked out everything else around her.

"Yet, when I went to the crime scene, there were two perfect bullet holes through the portrait of Holt Tierney hanging on the wall. You know of anything that can do that?"

The same corner of Hall's mouth turned up. He glanced to the bar. Raised his chin toward them.

The brother on the right turned back a moment. Took something up in his hand. Walked over to the table and slapped a pair of shiny brass cartridges down.

"Thanks, Hub," Hall said. Waited for the young man to retreat. Picked up one of the bullets and held it between his fingers for Drake to see.

"Tracer rounds," Hall said. "Bullets that aren't fired to kill, but to illuminate."

Drake accepted the bullet. Turned it over in his hands.

To his untrained eye, it looked no different than any other round he'd ever seen.

"How does it work?"

"The actual round, as you can see there, is a little smaller than your usual shell. Thinner, more elongated. The remainder of the jacket is filled with a phosphorescent powder. When the bullet is fired, the powder is released in a trail behind it.

"They're used to show where a target is, marking it for incoming support. Can be seen for miles around."

"And it throws off bright red light?" Drake asked. Looked up from the shell to Hall.

"Well, any color," Hall replied. "But yes, there are red shells for sure."

Pieces began to link up in Drake's mind. He rolled Hall's words around a moment. Coupled them with what he found at the Town Hall. What Wanda Pritchett had said.

"Not meant to kill, but illuminate," Drake said. Stared off for a moment. "Lukas Webb never had any intention of hurting anybody."

Drake snapped himself back to the present. Looked across at Hall. "He was making a point."

"It would appear that way, yes," Hall said.

"And whatever that was, it had everything to do with Holt Tierney."

Hall nodded in agreement. Said nothing.

CHAPTER TWENTY-EIGHT

Reconnaissance.

A slow pass by the hospital. By the catholic church.

An attempt to see if his ruse had worked.

For all intents and purposes, it seemed it had. McIlvaine's truck was nowhere to be seen as Drake eased past. Drove a full mile down the road. Turned around and returned just as slow in the opposite direction.

There were a handful of cars in the church parking lot, all on hand for the midweek Bible study advertised on the front sign.

None of them were trucks.

Drake pulled the Ranger into the lot. Parked between his truck and Rink's. Locked the doors and headed inside.

He found Rink and Sara both sitting in the hall outside Lukas's room. They were leaned in close to one another as he approached, whispering low.

They weren't touching, but something about their body language seemed to indicate they had been.

Or would be soon.

Drake made it a point to drag his feet across the floor as he approached to announce his presence. Make sure it didn't appear that he was interrupting anything.

At the sight of him, Rink stood up.

"Everything go alright?"

No sense of embarrassment. A definite tone of concern.

"It did," Drake said. "Switching vehicles threw him off my trail. He was gone when I came back."

"Sara said you went back out to see the Home Guard?"

Drake nodded. Leaned against the window on the opposite side of the hall. Folded his arms across his chest while facing them.

"I did. Found out a couple pieces of good information."

Rink remained standing. Cast a glance down to Sara.

She was perched on the edge of her seat, sleeves of her sweatshirt pulled down over her hands.

"Go ahead," Rink prompted.

"First, those guys do *not* like Hank McIlvaine. At all."

"Hank McIlvaine," Sara whispered. Made a face. Tried to place the name.

"The man who shot your brother," Drake said. Lowered his voice.

Sara's eyes slid shut. She nodded. "Of course."

"Why not?" Rink asked.

"Besides what he did to Lukas?" Drake said. "Apparently, he was a disgrace to the uniform. To this day draws medical benefits from some phantom injury."

Rink winced. "I'm guessing that goes over about as well as wiping his ass with the flag in that crowd."

Drake nodded. "Well put. I told them he was tailing us. Hall offered to take care of it."

A snort rolled out of Rink. "I bet he did. What did you tell him?"

"Asked him to hold off for the time being. Promised him once this was over, I'd disavow any knowledge the conversation ever took place.

"A promise, by the way, that now extends to you two as well."

Sara nodded in agreement.

Rink didn't acknowledge it. He didn't have to.

"Anything else?" Rink asked.

"You ever heard of a bullet called a tracer round?" Drake asked.

Sara shook her head. Looked up at Rink.

"Heard of it," Rink said. "Never used one."

"Well, that's one better than me," Drake said. "I spoke to Wanda Pritchett earlier today and she said the biggest thing she remembered from that night was light. Lots and lot of blinding red light."

"From the tracer rounds," Rink said. Began to pace in the hallway.

"Exactly," Drake said.

Sara leaned back in her chair. Folded her arms across her stomach.

"Okay, so what's the significance of that?"

"Hall told me that a tracer round isn't one meant to kill, but to illuminate. Lukas didn't go there that night to hurt anybody. He just wanted to be heard.

"When Tierney cut him off and wouldn't let him speak, he figured out another way to make a point."

Rink and Sara both accepted the information. Rink continued pacing. Sara remained motionless.

"So what was he trying to *illuminate?*" Rink asked. Made air quotes with his fingers as he spoke.

"Tierney," Drake said. "Kade and I went to the Town Hall yesterday. Lukas shot out the eyes of his picture on the wall. After that we went and talked to him. Guy couldn't give us an honest answer about anything."

"And his goon is now following you," Sara added.

Drake pointed a finger at her and nodded. "And now McIlvaine is following us."

Silence fell between them as a nurse shuffled by. Older and heavyset, she moved stiff and slow.

Eyed them as she passed.

"How is he?" Drake asked. Motioned with his chin toward the room.

Noticed the eye roll from the nurse as she departed.

Sara shifted in her seat. Faced the room behind her. Sighed.

"The same. The doctors say he should be ready to wake on Saturday. His vitals are stronger. His system will be able to withstand it."

Drake nodded, lowered his chin to his chest.

"Just so you know Sara, Pratt is still going to arrest him the moment he wakes up."

She turned back to face him. Her jaw dropped open.

"Did you see the Sheriff? Did he tell you anything?"

"Not since last weekend," Drake said. "But he and Goslin have both already stated their intentions publicly. They have to act now to save face."

"What if we get this figured out before then?"

"Won't matter," Drake said. "They'll arrest him anyway, just reduce the charges after the fact."

Sara lowered her gaze to the ground. Drew in deep breaths. Her lip began to quiver.

"Where will they take him?" Rink asked. Walked over to Sara. Placed a hand on her shoulder.

"Nowhere," Drake said. "Even if he's awake, he won't be fit to relocate. They'll just put him into custody. Return the guards here 24/7 until he's ready to move."

"So even if he gets arrested, he won't have to go to jail," Sara asked.

"Assuming we can get this figured out in time?" Drake asked. "No, he won't have to go to jail."

Another moment of silence passed.

Sara kept her head aimed down toward the ground. Took another deep breath. Looked at Drake with bloodshot eyes.

"Okay, so how do we get this figured out?"

Drake glanced to Rink. Saw the same determined look in his eyes.

"Do you have any idea, any at all, as to what Lukas was trying to say about Holt Tierney?"

Sara stared off at the far wall. Her lips moved a tiny bit as she repeated the question in silence. Tried to formulate an answer in her mind.

"No," she said. "I'm sorry, I don't. My role has always been in the house. Papa kept me pretty removed from the ranch business itself."

"Would he have shared it with Lukas?" Drake asked.

"I don't know," Sara said. Shook her head. "Maybe. Probably. Why?"

Rink noticed the look on Drake's face. Stood to full height.

Leveled his gaze on his friend.

"What are you thinking?"

"I'm thinking tomorrow I stay in Missoula and find out everything I can about brucellosis," Drake said. "That's what they were discussing in the meeting when things went sideways."

"And after that?" Rink asked.

Drake unfolded his arms. Shoved his hands deep in his pockets.

"Then I come back here on Saturday, and we ask Lukas what was going on with Holt Tierney."

CHAPTER TWENTY-NINE

Courthouse.

Not to be confused with the Town Hall, where Commission meetings were held.

The enormous brick edifice downtown that housed the official chambers used for all legal proceedings.

The Sheriff's Department.

The Ravalli County Attorney.

Everything needed for a legal case housed under one roof. From investigation to arrest to trial within yards of each other.

The last meeting of the afternoon on Paula Goslin's calendar was just down the hall. It was one she had been waiting on for two days now.

The heels on her patent leather boots clicked beneath her as she marched down the tiled hallway. She entered the Sheriff's office without knocking to find a young girl not far removed from high school sitting behind the desk.

The girl looked terrified as Goslin entered, pushing herself back away from the desk.

"Can I help you?" she asked. Revealed a mouth full of braces. Gums much too large for her teeth.

"Yes," Goslin said. Arched an eyebrow. "Please tell Sheriff Pratt I am here to see him."

The girl swallowed hard. Nodded up and down.

"And you are?"

"He knows who I am," Goslin said. Put more ice than necessary in her voice for effect.

The girl retreated from the desk and disappeared down the hall. Goslin stood for a moment and glanced around, taking in her surroundings.

Despite sharing space in the same building, their offices could not have been any different.

Goslin's favored bright colors and modern furniture. Straight lines. Clean angles.

This one looked more like a man cave.

Stuffed squirrels and pheasants. Tweed furniture. A lot of brown and green.

A smirk lifted one corner of her mouth as the girl emerged from the hallway.

"Sheriff Pratt said to please come on back. You know where it is?"

"I do," Goslin said. Left the young girl cowering behind her desk.

Her heels again sounded out through the office as she walked the length of the hall. Found the glass door with **Sheriff Jacob Pratt** stenciled on it. Knocked with the back of her knuckles.

"Come in," Pratt said from behind his desk. Stood as she entered. "Please, have a seat."

Goslin nodded in greeting. Settled into a brown tweed chair across from the Sheriff.

Glanced around to see his inner sanctum fit the motif of the outer office.

"Thank you for meeting with me," Goslin said. The frostiness of a few moments before was gone, though her tone was still a long way from convivial.

"Absolutely," Pratt said. "What can I do for you?"

Goslin fought hard to keep from rolling her eyes.

The Webb shooting was the biggest story to come out of Hamilton in almost a decade. Since the murder-suicide of a longtime resident eight years before.

"Lukas Webb," Goslin said. "Anything moving there?"

Pratt motioned down to a file sitting open on his desk. No more than three pieces of paper bound together by a metal clip.

"Not a lot to move," Pratt said. "Multiple witnesses saw Webb leave the meeting angry, return with a high-powered rifle, and begin shooting. He's still being held in a coma at Hamilton Memorial until Saturday."

"So Saturday is confirmed?" Goslin asked.

An oversized nod came back to her in response.

"I speak to his supervising physician each morning," Pratt said.

"Really?" Goslin said. Raised her eyebrows.

"Yes," Pratt said. "We both belong to the Crossroads Gym, see each other every day."

Goslin glanced down at the prodigious belly parked across from her. The way it strained the buttons on his shirt. Pressed against the desk.

The arch in her brow went a little higher. She said nothing.

"I've also asked that they contact us immediately should anything change."

"You're no longer keeping a guard posted there?"

"No," Pratt said. Shook his head. "Didn't have it in the budget for that kind of overtime. We'll go back to around-the-clock as soon as they wake him up."

Again, Goslin fought to hide an outward response. The most visible live criminal to come along in her lifetime, and the city was worried about paying out some overtime hours.

"I came down to let you know I have planned a press conference for Saturday afternoon," Goslin said. "I've asked for the local news station to be on hand from Missoula."

Pratt's eyes widened. "Really? For Saturday?"

"Yes," Goslin said. "I want it to take place right after he wakes and you arrest him. We need the state to see we are taking this very seriously."

A moment of silence passed as Pratt leaned back in his chair. Laced his fingers across his stomach.

A sheen of sweat appeared on his brow. His skin was pasty white.

"You seem to disagree," Goslin said. Put a touch of challenge in her voice.

"No," Pratt said. Twisted his head from side to side. "It's just...is that the best way for us to go?"

Goslin leaned forward. Rested her elbows on her knees. Let the fire shine behind her eyes.

"You have a better idea?"

"I'm not questioning you," Pratt said. "It's just, the man is a veteran. We have some pretty loyal people in this town. I'd hate to incense them if we don't have to."

"I agree," Goslin said. Nodded for effect. "But at the same time, we can't let people see that this sort of thing is acceptable, either. Veteran or not, the people in this town must be able to live free of fear."

Goslin cut herself off there. She was beginning to preach, which was something she didn't want to do.

There would be plenty of time for that in front of the cameras on Saturday.

"Have you considered offering to put him in state counseling?" Pratt asked. "I know they have some great programs for returning veterans over in Helena. Maybe this way justice is served, and we still appear sympathetic to those who serve our country."

Goslin scoffed. Leaned back in her chair. Straightened her blazer.

"This, coming from the man that ran a month ago on a Zero Tolerance platform?"

Pratt swallowed. Looked at her with sad eyes. Nodded.

"You're right. I just hate to see a young man with such a strong service record go away for the rest of his life over one mistake."

Goslin stared hard at him for a moment. Let her face soften as she gave a wan smile.

"I know. It is sad, and I agree with you. If there was any other way, we would pursue it. The fact is, this kid didn't make a mistake. He grabbed a rifle and started shooting up a civic meeting."

Silence fell once more as Pratt stared at her. Leaned forward and rested his elbows on the table.

"Is there anything you need from me at the press conference?"

CHAPTER THIRTY

Lights.

One in the living room. Another in the kitchen.

Drake saw them as he pulled up. Was quite certain he had not left them on that morning.

No cars out front. Garage door down.

The entire drive up from Hamilton was spent with one eye watching the rearview mirror. Upon reaching Missoula, he turned north up Reserve Street. Stopped off to pick up dinner.

Took the long way back around toward campus.

No sign of McIlvaine.

Drake drove past his home. Parked a few houses down on the street. Pulled out the tire iron from beneath his seat.

Moving fast, he walked up the sidewalk to his house. Tried to peek into the windows. Knew before looking that the shades were all down.

A habit due to the violent nature of the games Ajax was often working on.

Drake retreated away from the window. Tucked himself in behind a tree.

Pulled his cellphone from his pocket. Scrolled through the call log and hit send.

"Yo," Kade said after a single ring.

"Hey, where are you right now?"

"Home, why?" Kade said. Complete seriousness in his voice. "What's going on?"

"I've got lights on at the house," Drake said. "If you don't hear from me in 15 minutes, get over here."

Drake could hear movement on the other end of the line. "Is that guy back? You want me to come over now?"

"I don't see a car anywhere," Drake said. "Let me go in first. Maybe I just left some lights on in a hurry this morning."

"You never leave lights on," Kade said. "Let me get over there."

Drake peered around the tree at the house. Couldn't see or hear anything.

"Naw, let me go in here first. Give me 15 minutes."

"Ten," Kade replied. Hung up without a sound.

Drake crammed the phone back down into his pocket. Gripped the tire iron in his left hand. Went to the front door and shoved the key in with his right.

Pushed the door open and stepped inside, improvised weapon ready by his side.

Standing in the hallway, plate of food in hand, mouth agape, was Ajax.

"What the hell got into you?" Ajax asked.

Drake stood frozen a moment. Pushed out a sigh of relief as recognition set in. Smiled and lowered the tire iron.

"Good God, what the hell are you doing here?"

"Um, I live here," Ajax said. Walked around to an armchair. Set his food down on an end table. "What's got you so jumpy?"

"Long story," Drake said. Sighed again. Walked down the hall. Set the tire iron on the back of the couch.

"Damn," Ajax said. "Busting-into-the-house-carrying-a-tire-iron long story?"

"Yeah," Drake said. Circled around and dropped himself onto the couch.

"Who the hell did you expect to be here?" Ajax asked. Eyes still a bit wide.

"Hank McIlvaine," Drake said. Ran a hand over his face.

"The guy from TV the other night?" Ajax asked.

"Yeah," Drake said. "The one that shot Lukas Webb. He was tailing me around town earlier today."

"And you think he's coming here?" Ajax asked.

"No, not really. I lost him this afternoon," Drake said. "So, what are you doing back? I was going to pick you up Sunday from the airport."

Ajax leaned back in his chair. Let a sour look cross his face. Took up the plate of food from the table beside him.

"Couldn't do it. Four days was more than enough. Too damn much, as a matter of fact."

A smile curled up the corner of Drake's mouth.

"The girl? Or the family?"

"Yes," Ajax said. Shoveled a bite of potatoes into his mouth. "Damn, this is good. I should have just stayed here and gone to the Keuhl's with you."

"You should have," Drake said. "And please, eat all of it. I've had enough to last me a month."

A thought crossed Drake's mind. He fished his phone out and called Kade back.

Kade snatched up the phone mid-ring. "Everything alright?"

"Ajax."

"Ajax?" Kade spat. "I thought he was gone until Sunday?"

"Apparently, it was a train wreck. I'm just now getting the details myself."

"Ah hell. I take it he didn't end up getting his noodle wet?"

A smirk lifted Drake's head back toward the seat cushion behind him. "I think I'll let you ask him that tomorrow."

"That's right," Kade said. "We back up at the lodge in the morning?"

"We are," Drake said. "But I have to be done at 9:00. I want to be on campus by 10:00. Need to track down some folks."

"We'll be there," Kade said. Signed off.

"What's happening on campus tomorrow?" Ajax asked. Already had half the plate put down.

Drake tossed the phone onto the couch beside him. Leaned forward and scratched Q behind the ears.

157

"Have to speak with some people in the Ag Department. See what they can tell me about brucellosis."

"Is this something I don't want to hear about while I'm eating?" Ajax asked. Used a roll to sop up gravy.

Drake smiled. Shook his head. "All I know is it's a disease found in cattle. Hoping they can fill in the blanks for me tomorrow."

"This have anything to do with why you came storming through the front door carrying a tire iron?" Ajax asked.

A smile spread across Drake's face. He stood, headed toward the door.

"Don't know yet, but probably."

Ajax paused from eating a moment as he watched Drake go. "Where you headed now?"

"I'm going to get my truck and my dinner," Drake said. "Watching you eat is making me hungry."

CHAPTER THIRTY-ONE

Three.

McIlvaine was halfway through his third beer when the call came in.

The entirety of the conversation lasted less than a minute. Short. Terse.

Not a request. Not a suggestion.

A directive. Nothing short of a command.

Hank McIlvaine did not do well with commands.

Upon hanging up the phone, he finished his beer. Ordered a fourth and drank it slow.

Watched a couple of unknown college football teams play in a third-tier bowl game on the TV above the bar.

When his beer was gone, he rose. Laid a $20 down. Nodded to the barkeep. Went to his truck and headed toward the Tierney Ranch.

A full 30 minutes after getting the call, he pulled up in front of the farm house. Saw only a single light on in the back.

Knew it to be Tierney's home office. Knew he was the only one awake.

McIlvaine turned on his high beams. Blasted his music as loud as it would go. Pulled the nose of his truck up as close to the house as he could.

Made sure the light and noise both filled the home before shutting them off.

Fueled half by anger, half by liquid courage, he exited the truck and slammed the door hard. Walked across the front porch and raised his fist to announce his presence with authority.

The door swung open before he got the chance.

Behind it stood Tierney, fuming. Eyes pinched in tight. Cheeks flushed red.

"What the hell are you doing? I told you to be quiet, my wife was sleeping."

Anger permeated the words. They came out clipped, short. Nothing more than a harsh whisper.

"I thought I was," McIlvaine replied. Did his best to keep from smiling.

"And where the hell have you been?" Tierney muttered. "I called you a half-hour ago."

"Yeah, I was in the middle of something."

Tierney pulled back an inch. Glared. "A six-pack, right?"

Before McIlvaine could respond, a sleepy voice called down from the second floor.

"Holt? Is everything okay?"

Tierney leveled a withering glare on McIlvaine.

"Everything's fine, Dear. Go back to bed."

"Are you sure? What's going on down there?"

Tierney again stared hard at his visitor.

"Nothing. Go back to sleep."

The two men waited as the sound of Bernice's footsteps faded away. The scowl remained in place as Tierney jerked his head toward the back. Led McIlvaine through the house to his home office.

"Do I even want to know what that stunt was all about?" Tierney asked. Settled in behind his desk. Steepled his fingers before him.

"Wasn't a stunt," McIlvaine said. Shook his head to the side. Dropped himself into an armchair on the opposite side of the desk. "You called, I came over."

Tierney paused a moment. Glared.

Let it pass.

"The reason I called you here tonight is, we've got a situation."

McIlvaine waited for him to continue. Said nothing.

"As you know, Bret Greeley has been field testing our herd over the course of the last few weeks."

"I'm aware."

Tierney pushed on without acknowledging the comment.

"Earlier today, he found two more. That makes a total of five."

McIlvaine gave a twist of the head. "Five out of 5,000 isn't too bad."

A loud snort rolled out of Tierney. A derisive twist of the head accompanied it. "That's why you work for me. *Any* out of 5,000 is too many. Do you know how hard the state is cracking down on this stuff right now?"

"Apparently not," McIlvaine said. Sighed. Rolled his gaze up to the elk on the wall above them.

Tierney followed his stare upward. Latched onto the elk as well.

Just as fast, McIlvaine returned his attention to the meeting. Under no uncertain terms did he want or need to hear the story of the elk again.

Every time it got a little bigger. A little more salacious.

It wouldn't be long and the old man would be saying he ran it down on foot. Ripped its throat out with his teeth.

"So why do we care?" McIlvaine asked. "Or better yet, why do *I* care?"

The old man shifted his attention back down. Let the scowl return.

Whether it was at being cut off before he could tell his story or at the comment, McIlvaine wasn't sure.

"We care because this is big. Could bring down the whole ranch."

McIlvaine stared unblinking back at him. Said nothing.

"That's several million dollars in total assets. Over a dozen jobs," Tierney added. Had the same dark red flush return to his cheeks.

Again, McIlvaine remained silent.

Stayed that way until the old man leaned back in his seat. Slowed his breathing a touch.

"Okay," McIlvaine finally replied. "So you need them to disappear. Same thing that happened with the other three?"

"No," Tierney said. Remained reclined in his chair. Rubbed the back of his right hand with his left. "These two just need to disappear."

McIlvaine nodded in response.

"You care how or where?"

"Not particularly. Just make sure the brand is destroyed and the tag removed. Nothing that can trace them back to us."

Another nod.

"So what's the difference between these two and the three before?"

Tierney stopped rubbing his hand. His eyes hardened as he stared at McIlvaine.

"The first two were to serve a purpose. The third was because the situation changed. Now, we have no reason to go further. Any more would just be overkill."

Confusion played across McIlvaine's face.

Tierney gave him a dismissive wave. "Just make them go away. That's all that matters right now."

Once more, McIlvaine fought down the urge to roll his eyes. To stand and walk out. To spit at the old man.

To come flying across the desk and split his sanctimonious face open. "When?"

"How many have you had tonight?" Tierney asked.

"Two," McIlvaine lied.

Tierney nodded. "They're waiting for you in the auxiliary barn as we speak."

He extended a piece of paper across the desk. Two non-sequential numbers were written in black ink.

"These are the numbers."

McIlvaine took the paper. Glanced at it. Nodded. Stood.

He made it almost to the door.

"Oh, and Hank?"

McIlvaine turned. Glanced sideways at the profile of the old man staring out the window. "Yeah?"

"Try and keep that damn music off until you're away from the house. Woman's a bear to live with when she doesn't get her sleep."

CHAPTER THIRTY-TWO

Jet lag.

Street slang for desynchronosis.

A physiological condition resulting from air travel. Crossing time zones. The disruption of circadian rhythms.

Also, Ajax's excuse for getting annihilated on the final run of the morning. Beaten so badly that it nullified Kade's first place finish.

Allowed Sage and Drake to win breakfast free of charge once more.

The crowd in Snow Plaza was a bit heavier than a week prior. Maybe three to five extra people. Students back a little early from break.

No faces that stood out to the Zoo Crew as they entered.

In the corner, Lewis and Cynthia Hill both stuck a hand in the air. Received a quartet of waves in response.

No attempt at conversation from either side.

There were plenty of reasons to be jovial this morning.

An empty Snow Plaza. Ski runs that remained pristine all morning. New Year's Eve just two days away.

None of those seemed to matter to the Crew as they entered. None were openly angry. None especially joyous, either.

Kade went first, walking fast. Kept his gaze aimed downward.

Muttered as he went about winning the race and still having to shell out for breakfast.

Halfway across the floor, he flagged down Helen standing by the kitchen. Asked for the usual.

Got a thumb up in response.

Behind him was Drake and Sage.

Drake too kept his eyes aimed downward. Tried to make sense of the case. Determine what he hoped to gain by his trip to campus.

To his right, Sage sensed the general demeanor of the group. The relative quiet of the entire morning.

Not hostility. Everyone just tending to keep to themselves.

Making up the rear was Ajax. Shaking his head. Sputtering sentence fragments about jet lag. Keeping most of his snow gear on.

The table was subdued as all four sat down around it. Peeled off their hats and gloves. Avoided eye contact as they stared down at nothing.

Sage was the first one brave enough to wade in.

She always was.

"Well, this is fun," she said. Piled her hat atop a pair of Gore-Tex gloves.

It took a full moment for the comment to resonate with the table. Kade glanced over at her. Ajax burrowed deeper into his coat.

Drake raised his gaze from the table.

"Sorry. Mind's not in it this morning."

"Yeah, what's going on here?" Ajax asked. "Last night, you busted in swinging a crowbar. Today you haven't said a word."

Sage turned her attention to Drake. Narrowed her eyes.

"You came in swinging a crowbar?"

A smile tugged at the corner of Drake's mouth. "No. It was a tire iron. And I wasn't swinging anything. More like holding it, just in case."

"In case of what?" Kade asked. Pulled the tie out of his hair. Twisted his head to let it swing down around his shoulders.

Drake extended his hands out over the table. Locked his fingers and stretched. "Yesterday, the guy that shot Lukas Webb three times started tailing me. Call me crazy, but..."

"Crazy," Ajax said.

After a moment, he broke into a smile. Swatted at Drake with a glove. Pulled his hat off. Let his dreadlocks stay in a tangle atop his head.

"So we're going there?" Drake asked, smiling. "How about we proceed to the pink elephant in the room?"

Kade and Sage both smiled. Matched Drake's stare at Ajax.

"What pink elephant?" Ajax asked, feigning ignorance.

"Why the hell you're back here now instead of still home in Boston?" Kade asked.

A heavy eye roll was Ajax's response. He unzipped his coat and let it hang free around his torso. Shook his head from side to side. Muttered in disgust.

"Y'all are worse than a bunch of schoolgirls, you know that?"

"And when it's one of us, you're the worst one," Sage said.

"Amen, sister," Kade added. "How many cracks have I heard at my expense about my late night activities?"

Ajax's mouth dropped open. He looked at Kade. Over to Drake.

"Help me out here?"

"Hey, you're on your own," Drake said. Raised his hands by his side. Shook his head. "But, to be fair, Kade's late night activities are a bit legendary."

Pure indignation spread over Kade's face.

"Are you kidding me right now? We have a prime opportunity to go after Ajax and you come my way?"

"Nobody's going after you," Sage said. "But you kind of left yourself open with that comment...and your – ahem – late night activities."

Chuckles went up from both Ajax and Drake.

"But," Drake said. Steered the conversation back on course. "Before we get too far astray, let's bring this back around. Lord knows we'll have many, many...many opportunities to discuss Kade's nightlife."

Kade offered a middle finger salute in Drake's direction.

Stifled laughter shook Sage's entire body as she fought not to make a sound.

Drake ignored them both.

"Ajax, to what do we owe the pleasure of your company this fine morning?"

"I don't want to talk about it," Ajax said.

Received stony stares from all three.

One at a time he looked around the table. Found no quarter from any of them.

"Alright, fine," he said. Smacked his hands against his thighs. "I couldn't take it anymore. Had to get out of there."

"Couldn't take what?" Sage asked. Leaned forward and rested her elbows on the table.

"This time, my mother tried to employ a new trick for getting me to move back," Ajax said.

"You've already got money, so that only leaves women," Kade said. Gave a knowing nod.

"No, it doesn't," Sage said. Rolled her eyes at her brother. "Not everyone is wired like you. What did she try?"

"Women," Ajax deadpanned. Drew a laugh from Drake. Clapping from Kade. "And again, I don't want to talk about it."

"I told you!" Kade said. Rocked his body from side to side in his chair.

Drake pressed a fist to his mouth. Closed his eyes tight as his upper body trembled with laughter.

"So what was the problem?" Sage asked. Ignored the others around her. Focused in on Ajax, silhouetted by the fireplace behind him.

"I said I don't want to talk about it," Ajax said. Same sour expression back in place.

"Oh, come on," Kade said. "Don't punk out on us now."

"Not your type?" Drake asked.

"An old flame?" Sage asked.

"No, wait, let me guess," Kade said. Extended an arm across the table to Drake and Sage. "I bet she was hefty, wasn't she?"

"No, she wasn't hefty!" Ajax spat. Voice so high it was almost a yell. Drew stares from the handful of patrons in the lodge. "She was on the payroll!"

The moment the words left his mouth, a look of regret splashed across Ajax's face.

He glanced the length of the room. Stared down at his lap. Shook his head from side to side.

Looked up to see the other three members of the Crew sitting with matching expressions.

Eyes wide. Mouths agape. Motionless.

"Your parents tried to bribe you with a hooker?" Drake asked. Drew out each word slow and deliberate.

Again, Ajax looked the length of the room.

"No," he muttered. "They found some girl and incentivized her to act interested. Thought I might be into her, get me to come around more. Maybe even move back."

The silence continued. The looks of pure shock.

"So when you say she *employed* a new tactic..." Drake mumbled.

After a moment, Kade snorted. Followed it with a low chuckle.

Unable to hold it in, Sage followed suit. Drake was just a step behind.

Ajax stared down at his hands as long as he could before a crack of white creased his face.

The smile grew as he looked up. Took in his friends giggling. Joined them.

By the time their breakfast arrived, their laughter filled the entire end of Snow Plaza. Echoed off the walls.

Brought smiles to the faces of all others present.

CHAPTER THIRTY-THREE

Fish and Wildlife Biology.

The only true Agriculture program in the state was at Montana State University.

Bozeman.

Three hours and a treacherous drive across Homestake Pass outside of Butte. Six and two counting the way back.

Drake had neither the time or inclination to make such a trip. Didn't know anybody at MSU that would make a phone conference possible.

Instead, the afternoon before he had scrolled through the University of Montana campus directory. Made a few phone inquiries. Explained who he was and what he was looking for.

Made a few more phone calls.

It took over an hour to set something concrete.

The first three numbers he called were out of the office for the holidays. The next two stated brucellosis was well outside their field of study.

The sixth caller just scoffed and hung up.

Not until the seventh call, just one up from the end of his list, did Drake strike pay dirt. He had no idea what or who to expect when he showed up, but from the sound of the man's voice, he was excited to help.

If nothing else, Drake had a feeling he wouldn't be bored.

The lot around campus was deserted as Drake pulled his truck to a stop in front of the biology department. Hung his school-issued parking decal from the rearview mirror. Took up his shoulder bag and climbed out.

A vicious gust of wind blew through the Hellgate Canyon as he exited. Whipped through his jeans and hooded sweatshirt. Rattled the barren tree limbs above him.

Shoulders bunched high, he turned his back on the gale and headed for the front door. Ignored the passing glance of a co-ed powerwalking to her car.

Entered the plain red brick building on the corner of campus 10 minutes before their agreed meeting time.

A plume of steamy air washed over him as he stepped through the frosted glass doors. Hit his cold skin. Brought a rush of blood to the surface.

Stamping his feet, he walked into the building and headed for the nearest stairwell. Took it up to the second floor. Followed the directions he was given the day before.

Found the office he was looking for tucked away at the end of the hall.

The door stood open as he approached, *Seven Bridges Road* by the Eagles pouring out.

An involuntary smile crossed his face as he paused a moment. Let the song take him back to his father working in the garage. Singing off-tune.

Trying to convince anyone that would listen that his voice harmonized perfectly with those of Don Henley and Glenn Frey.

Using the back of his hand, Drake knocked twice. Walked into a room that was part-lab, part-office.

No signs of life anywhere.

"Hello?"

The music kicked off. The sound of boxes moving about could be heard. A moment later, a barrel-chested man emerged.

Red hair. Thick beard. Grey thermal. Cowboy khakis.

Top of a head that barely came to Drake's chin.

He smiled as he approached. Stuck a meaty paw out in front of him.

"Morning, Chase Riley. Associate Professor, department lightning rod, family black sheep,."

Deep, bombastic voice.

"Good morning, Drake Bell, law student in dire need of some answers."

He wasn't sure what made him open with the line. Decided to go with it anyway.

"You and me both, Brother. Get you something to drink?"

"No, thank you," Drake said. "Appreciate you meeting with me here this morning."

Riley pulled a pair of wooden stools over. Slid one in front of Drake. Perched himself atop the other. Hooked his feet on the rungs at the bottom.

"Hey, you said the magic word. I'm always happy to talk to anybody that wants to listen about brucellosis."

Drake smiled. "Then it sounds like I've come to the right place."

Riley nodded. Dug his beefy fingers into his beard. Scratched. "That you have. So what's your interest with Bang's?"

"Bang's?" Drake asked.

"Bang's disease," Riley said. "Contagious abortion, Malta fever. All different ways for saying brucellosis."

"Ah," Drake said. Thought about taking out his pad to write down notes. Decided against it.

Something told him this was best served as a free flowing conversation.

"A client of mine recently had a dust-up with his local Agriculture Commission. They were discussing brucellosis when things got a little hairy."

Riley nodded. Grunted. "Yeah, has a way of doing that. You have any idea what in particular it was that tripped him up?"

For a moment, Drake debated continuing the ruse. Playing it vague.

Opted to go straight ahead. Riley was doing him a solid. He needed to reciprocate.

"No," Drake said. "He's been in a coma since the incident, so I haven't been able to ask."

A knowing look settled over Riley's face. He studied Drake a moment. Nodded. "Hamilton?"

Drake matched the stare. "You've heard?"

"Everybody has. It true that boy was a veteran?"

"Home less than two weeks," Drake said.

Once more Riley nodded. Folded his thick arms across his chest. "Just ain't right. You ask, I'll answer. That work?"

Drake removed his phone from his pocket. Wagged it at Riley. "You mind if I record this? I don't want to miss anything, don't want to spend the whole time taking notes."

A wave of the hand signaled for Drake to continue. He set the phone to record and placed it on the corner of a nearby table.

"Alright, let's start at the beginning," Drake said. "What is brucellosis?"

Riley nodded. "Now, before we get started, you should know that I am pro-agriculture. Big-time. So what I say might be a bit stilted. That okay?"

"That's perfect," Drake said. Nodded.

"Alright, then. Brucellosis is a disease mostly found in bovines. Cows, elk, bison. It's caused by the bacteria *brucella* and causes aborted fetuses, weak calves, uterine infections, even arthritic joints."

"Nasty stuff."

Drake nodded. He wasn't intimately familiar with cattle production, but knew enough to process what Riley was telling him.

None of which was good.

"So it's a bacteria? Can hit anywhere?"

Riley made an noncommittal face. Scrunched up the left side. Wagged a hand on edge.

"Yes and no. It is a bacteria, sure, but it isn't that indiscriminate. It doesn't just occur, it has to be passed around. Usually that's through bodily fluids of an infected animal."

"So one cow becomes infected, aborts a fetus, other animals in the herd get infected?" Drake asked.

"Again, in principal, yes," Riley said, "but it's rarely that straightforward. Most of the time, cows actually contract it from elk that wander into their grazing area. They'll drop fluids, later a cow will eat that grass..."

Drake winced.

"So elk are the biggest source of spreading the disease?"

"Elk and bison," Riley said. "Bison over around Yellowstone, up near Bison National Park. Elk in other places, just because they have so much more room to roam."

"So there's really nothing they can do to stop the spread?" Drake asked. "I mean, it's not like anybody can catch and vaccinate elk in the wild."

Again, Riley gave a back and forth twist of his head. "Right, but some efforts have been made. Mostly it's through vaccination of cattle, but there's been some pretty serious headway made on the wildlife side as well."

Drake nodded. "Okay, give me a ballpark here. How effective are we talking?"

The corners of Riley's lips curled up beneath his thick red beard.

"Confession number two, this is part of what I do here. Helping to develop new vaccines."

"Oh, wow," Drake said. Cast a look around. Took in the scads of work stations around the room. Microscopes. Incubators. Charts and graphs on the wall.

"I'm guessing you've been pretty successful?"

Riley bowed the top of his head. "In the '50s, there were well over 100,000 herds affected. Cost livestock producers north of $400,000,000. Lost beef product. Decreased milk production. Everything."

"And today?" Drake asked.

He had no idea how any of this might tie into the Webb's. At the moment, he didn't much care.

"Six herds in the entire country that we know about. Less than $1,000,000 in total damages."

A low, shrill whistle passed through Drake's lips. He leaned back. Rolled his gaze toward the ceiling.

Contemplated the information.

"That's impressive."

"It's been a long time doing," Riley confessed.

Silence fell for a moment as the two men chewed on the numbers. Contemplated their impact.

"So, there's pretty regular monitoring of cows for brucellosis?" Drake asked.

"Oh yeah," Riley said. "Makes steroids testing in sports look like child's play by comparison. For dairy cows, milk is tested every quarter. For beef animals, a blood test before slaughter."

"Every single animal?" Drake asked.

"Ahh, the million dollar question," Riley said. Again rubbed his beard. Stared at the wall behind Drake for a moment.

"The short answer is, it depends on where you live."

A look of confusion passed over Drake's face. His mouth pinched into a tight circle. His eyes went wide.

He said nothing. Sat and waited for Riley to continue.

"The long answer is, Montana is a two-tier state. Tier One is for ranches inside what they call a designated zone. Basically, the area right around the Park."

"Where most of the bison and elk are?" Drake asked.

"Right," Riley said. Jabbed a finger at him. Nodded. "If you live in there, you have to get every last animal tested annually.

"In Tier Two - the rest of the state - you only have to have a certain percentage tested. And even then, only if they are going to slaughter."

"Much less invasive," Drake commented.

"Hell of a lot cheaper, too," Riley said. "That's the bigger thing. Most of these guys want to know if they have infected livestock, but they don't want the time or expense of having to load them all up to get tested all the time."

"Ouch," Drake agreed. "Seems like a raw deal for the folks in Tier One."

"It is," Riley said. "But not just them. Anybody in Tier Two with a positive test is now subject to quarantine. Has to get their entire herd tested for three years thereafter.

"That's a new regulation, has plenty of people up in arms around the state."

"I bet," Drake said. Nodded. Let his gaze pass to the windows along the wall for a moment.

Outside, a thin spray of snow was beginning to fall. Drake watched as the wind whipped it past the window. Against the thick boughs of a pine tree.

"So, aside from being a direct threat to a rancher's livelihood-" Drake said. Was cut off before he could get any further.

"It absolutely is," Riley said. Nodded for emphasis. "You get hit the wrong time of year and have your herd quarantined, you could be in real trouble. Not to mention the enormous cost and pain in the ass of testing."

Drake smirked at Riley's frank assessment. Pushed forth with the remainder of his question.

"Aside from that though, what direct threat does brucellosis cause?"

Riley smacked his leg. Shook his head from side to side.

"I'm such an idiot sometimes. I forgot the damn punchline. The real concern is that it can be passed on to humans."

Drake's jaw dropped open. He stared across at Riley. Waited for him to continue.

"That's right," Riley said. Saw Drake's response and smirked. "People that come in contact with fluids, tainted meat, anything, are also susceptible."

A shudder ran the length of Drake's spine. He paused a moment. Worked his tongue around inside his mouth. Tried to form some saliva.

"How bad?"

Riley held up a hand. Pressed his thumb and forefinger together. Began there and switched to a new finger with each symptom he rattled off.

"Fever, chills, sweats, joint pains. Backache, weight loss, reduced appetite. It's nothing to be taken lightly, for sure."

Drake ran through the list in his mind.

"Could it be fatal?"

"Not often," Riley said. "But not unheard of. Anytime you have a disruption of the body's equilibrium, it is possible."

One last question crept into the back of Drake's mind. Part of him didn't want to ask it. The rest knew he'd be remiss if he left without addressing it.

He wouldn't be doing Lukas or Sara right if he didn't.

"Let me ask you this," Drake said. "If a major producer found brucellosis in his herd, how far might he go to cover it up?"

Riley looked right back at him. Paused a moment. Shook his head to the side.

"Best guess? As far as he had to."

CHAPTER THIRTY-FOUR

Twenty-two hours.

In a week, Sara had left Hamilton Memorial Hospital for a total of 22 hours.

The first two nights, she spent sleeping in the chair beside Lukas's bed. The next three, she went home to catch four fitful hours. Shower. Head back in.

The other 10 hours were scattered over the course of seven days.

A quick trip out to the farm to speak with their only employee, Louis Malten. De facto ranch manager for the time being.

A couple of quick food runs.

A shower each morning.

The remainder of the time she spent in or nearby Lukas's room.

The bulk of her adult life had been spent tied to the ranch. Cooking meals for her father and Louis. Doing endless loads of laundry.

Helping with branding. Calving. Vaccinating.

When Lukas left eight years before, she became an indispensable part of the operation. Deep down, she always feared her father would have rather had another boy to help work the ranch.

Spent her days determined to prove she was just as capable as her brother.

Despite that, there was always a disconnect. Something that told her she wasn't quite on the level with her father and Lukas.

She was good enough to help work the fields. Run irrigation lines. Move cows to summer pasture.

Not once had she ever seen the company books.

Even in his death, her father had been explicit in his will. That part of the operation was to be handled by Lukas.

Now that her father was gone, Lukas was in a coma, her world had narrowed to the confines of the hospital.

There was no doubt work she could be doing. Needed to be doing. But she couldn't bring herself to leave.

They were a fairly small operation. Enough to provide for the family. Pay Louis.

It was nothing one man couldn't handle on his own for a week.

Right after the meeting, Sara was back in the hospital. The staff had long since given up trying to move her along.

Most of the place cleared out right at 5:00. Friday before a long holiday weekend. Only essential staff on hand.

By 10:00, it was deserted.

Sara walked the halls alone for over an hour. Smiled at a handful of people. Kept her gaze aimed down, watching the overhead light reflect off the tile floor.

Let her mind wander.

Tried to connect the dots between what the Sheriff told her about the incident. What Drake had found. What she knew about Lukas.

Wondered about what would happen the next morning.

If there would be a large public spectacle. If Lukas's body could take the pressure of waking up.

She sensed something different the moment she rounded the last corner. Saw the shadow pass across the open doorway to Lukas's room.

Gone were any of the things she'd been chewing on just a moment before. In their place was a single thought.

It was not uncommon for a nurse to swing by on occasion and check things.

Not once had they done it without turning the lights on.

Sara's mouth went dry. Her steps reduced to six inches at a time as she crept forward. Pushed a hand into the pocket of her sweatshirt.

Made sure her cellphone was still in place.

Swinging wide, she came up on the far side of the hallway. Peered into the room.

Saw nothing.

The hair at the nape of her neck stood on end as she inched forward. Tried to run her tongue over her lips. Drew in shallow breaths through her nose.

Crept to the edge of the room.

In the half-darkness, she could see Lukas lying in bed. Hear the same rhythmic sounds of his breathing apparatus and heart rate monitor.

"Hello?" she whispered. Took two steps into the room.

The blow hit her full in the shoulder.

Body-to-body contact that lifted her into the air. Tossed her against the door standing open. Deposited her on the ground in a heap.

Stars danced in front of her eyes. The air was driven from her lungs.

Between gasps, Sara rolled onto her stomach. Heard the sound of boots slapping against tile.

She pushed herself out into the hallway just far enough to see the back of a man running away. Nothing more than a glimpse before disappearing.

Body on fire, Sara pressed her cheek flat against the floor. Let the cool tile soothe her skin.

Fought to slow her heartrate. To regain normal breathing.

After a few moments, she pushed herself to a seated position. Fished her phone from the pouch in her sweatshirt.

Typed out a quick text message and hit send.

Get here. Now.

CHAPTER THIRTY-FIVE

Forty seconds.

That was the only difference between Rink pulling into the parking lot of Hamilton Memorial and Drake right behind him.

Rink was the first one out. Held a stainless steel wrench with a two-inch head in his hand. Stood and stared at Drake's truck.

Relaxed as he realized who it was. Tossed the implement into the bed of his truck.

Drake emerged to hear the sound of metal-on-metal contact.

"I saw your headlights behind me the whole way down," Rink said. "Thought for a minute I might have a tail, too."

"I figured that was you," Drake said. Fell in beside Rink. Walked together for the door. "Couldn't imagine anybody else that would drive fast enough I never caught them."

"Actually, I laid off the gas just a bit hoping you were following me," Rink said.

Didn't explain further. Didn't have to.

"What do you know?" Drake asked. Ignored the statement. Focused them back to their reason for being there.

"Nothing," Rink said. Shook his head in disgust. "You?"

Drake gave a twist of the head. Stepped through the double door. Headed toward the intensive care ward.

"Same. I got a text from her an hour ago. I tried hitting her back, but she's gone silent."

"Yeah," Rink said. Nodded. "We had a game tonight or I would have been here."

The last sentence came out almost as an apology.

Drake nodded at the statement. Said nothing.

No words of condolences were going to help anything right now. They both felt guilty. No point trying to avoid it.

They rounded a corner and came into view of Lukas's room at the same time.

Sara sat in a chair in the hallway outside, leaning forward, chewing on a thumbnail. Staring at nothing on the opposite wall.

A short distance down the hall, a uniformed deputy loitered. Young guy. Short-cropped hair. Looked no more than a week removed from the Academy.

His body tensed as Drake and Rink approached, his hand reaching for his hip.

Just as fast, he went slack as Sara saw them. Stood in greeting.

Drake eased up a half-step as they approached. Made sure Rink was the first to arrive.

Watched as he wrapped Sara in an oversized hug. Pulled back after a moment. Ran his hands down either side of her face. Cupped her chin.

"What happened? Are you okay? Is Lukas?"

Drake stood by in silence. It was as he had suspected all along.

Sara's eyes were red and puffy, the rims of her nostrils raw. Still, her face was dry as she looked up at Rink.

Over to Drake.

"There was someone here. Someone in the room with Lukas."

The words came out low, just above a whisper.

As the last one came out, her face crinkled. Shoulders lifted with a shudder.

"Shh," Rink said. Led her down to the chair. Sat in the one beside it. Laid a hand on her back. "It's okay, we're here now. What happened?"

Sara sniffled several more moments. Wiped her face with the cuff of her sweatshirt. Looked up at each of them.

"Two hours ago, I decided to go for a walk." She motioned with a hand toward the empty hallway. "As you can see, there's nobody here. Just wanted to stretch my legs for a minute."

Drake and Rink both listened in silence.

"When I came back, I don't know why, but I just had this feeling that something was wrong. I got a little closer and saw a shadow in the reflection in the window there."

She motioned with her chin toward the glass behind Drake.

"I came in to see if Lukas was okay. Barely made it inside before someone tackled me, knocked me against the door."

Drake could see the knuckles on Rink's hand grow white beneath his skin.

Felt the same hostility rise within him.

"Who was it?" Drake asked. Voice low. Thick. "Were you able to get a look at him?"

Sara shook her head. Sniffed. "No. He knocked me to the ground. I rolled out in time to see him running down the hall, but that was all."

Silence fell over the group.

Drake chewed at his bottom lip. Added the story to the facts he'd been running through his head since leaving Missoula.

Rink raised his gaze to Drake. Said what they were both thinking.

"It's got to be him."

"It does," Drake agreed.

Drake shifted his attention to the young deputy pacing at the end of the hall. Watched as he pretended not to be glancing over at them.

"I'll be back," Drake said. Walked down toward the deputy.

The guy stopped pacing, looking like he might vomit or open fire as Drake approached.

"Evening," Drake said. Let his southern drawl climb out slow and easy.

"Evening," the young man replied. A brass nameplate on his coat revealed his last name to be Kellogg.

His gaze flicked from Drake to Rink and Sara. Back again.

He had thick brown hair mashed from being beneath his hat. Hollow cheeks. Pale skin without a single bit of facial stubble.

"You family?" Kellogg asked.

"He's family," Drake said. Motioned over his shoulder. "I'm a friend. And their lawyer."

Kellogg's Adam's Apple bobbed as he swallowed.

"You guys been able to track down anything yet?" Drake asked.

Again, Kellogg looked at him, to Rink and Sara sitting nearby. Seemed to decide whatever he was debating in his mind.

"Looks like one guy, white, posing as a janitor. Came in pushing a broom, went into Lukas Webb's room. A few minutes later, Sara Webb arrived and scared him off."

Drake nodded, processing the information.

"So she wasn't the primary target."

Not a question. A realization.

Kellogg shook his head. "We don't think so. It looks like whoever it was targeted Lukas. She just happened to come along before anything could occur."

Another nod from Drake. He turned and glanced to see Rink looking back at him. Sara staring at the opposite wall.

He looked up into the corner. Motioned to the white camera mounted on a miniature pedestal.

"Able to pull anything at all from there?"

Kellogg's mouth drew into a tight line as he shook his head. "Not really. White male. Average height and build. He had a hat pulled low as he approached. Was running away from the camera as he left."

Average height and build. Fit with Drake's recollection of McIlvaine.

"Any of the other cameras?"

Another twist of the head. "Nothing clear. The guy knew what he was doing. Stayed in dark spots, kept his face hidden."

Drake nodded.

Disappointed, but not surprised.

A few other questions came to mind. Tinged with anger, there was no way to ask them without sounding accusatory.

Drake opted to let them pass.

"Thanks," Drake said. "We'll be here all night if anything comes up, please."

Kellogg nodded. Exhaled. Looked relieved.

"Will do."

Drake left him at the end of the hall. Returned to his spot across from Rink and Sara. Leaned against the wall. Shoved his hands in his pockets.

"Anything?" Rink asked.

Drake pursed his lips. Shook his head.

"Very little. One guy, white, medium height and weight."

"Sounds like him," Rink said. Bit more vitriol around the edges.

"Could be," Drake conceded. Retreated back into his thoughts. Let the gnawing ideas from the recesses of his mind come together.

Form a cohesive plan.

His eyes glazed over as he tried to draw a linear connection between everything that was happening. Tried to coalesce everything he'd learned in the last few days.

"Where you at right now?" Rink asked.

Drake blinked himself alert.

"Just thinking," Drake said.

Sara glanced up. Focused her attention on him.

"About?" Rink asked.

Drake looked over at Sara. Nudged his chin at the door behind her.

"What time are they scheduled to wake Lukas?"

A puff of air passed over Sara's lips. Her eyes grew a bit wider as she looked up at him.

"Um, 10:00. Why?"

Drake nodded, did the math backward in his head.

A little less than 10 hours. After a week, it bore to reason there wouldn't be much difference.

"If we got the doctor to agree to wake him now, would you sign off on it?"

CHAPTER THIRTY-SIX

Solumedrol.

Fancy name for hydrocortisone.

Reversing agent of choice for medically-induced comas.

Raises blood pressure. Increases metabolism. Uses the body's natural processes to regain consciousness.

The attending physician wasn't crazy about the idea of waking Lukas early.

Not that the loss of 10 hours would have any harmful effect. More that she knew his primary physician wanted to be the one to do it.

Be on hand when the Sheriff's department walked in. Answer any questions that might arise.

Stand in front of the flashbulbs.

Drake and Sara were prepared to wait until morning if the doctor gave a valid medical reason for doing so. Were not about to stand around so a small-town doc could have his moment in the sun.

The attending laughed when they told her their decision. Made sure they went on the record as stating she had cautioned them to wait.

Injected the reversing agent. Removed his breathing tube. Put him under an oxygen mask.

Told them it would be an hour or two before Lukas was awake and coherent.

Turned out she was right on both fronts.

An hour after the chemical went into his IV, Lukas's eyes fluttered open. Stared at the ceiling. Made no attempt to focus.

Beside him, Sara sat on the edge of her seat. Gripped his hand in both hers. Ignored the tears dripping off her chin.

In the doorway stood Drake and Rink.

Both unmoving. Both silent.

A half hour after his eyes opened, Lukas pulled the mask aside. Resumed breathing on his own.

Winced a few times with the effort.

Tried to mumble something incoherent. Was told by Sara to wait.

Two hours after the reversing agent was administered, Lukas raised his hands to his eyes. Wiped the crusted sleep from them.

Shook his head from side to side.

"Holy shit," he muttered. "What happened?"

New tears streamed down Sara's face as she sat beside him. Tried to respond. Gave up, lowered her face toward the floor and cried.

Lukas looked past her to Rink and Drake in the doorway. His face crinkled into confusion.

"Rink?"

Rink raised his chin upward in salute. "Hey man, how you feeling?"

Lukas ignored the question. Shifted his gaze to Drake.

"And...I don't know you, do I?"

"No," Drake said. Shook his head.

The look of confusion grew a bit deeper. "Army?"

"Friend of Rink's," Drake replied. "Your lawyer."

The words pushed Lukas's head back against his pillow. His eyes toward the ceiling overhead. "Damn. If I need a lawyer, that means it all really happened, didn't it?"

Sara raised her head. Nodded. Started to cry again.

Lukas raised a hand and wrapped it around the back of her head. Stroked her hair.

"Shh," he whispered. "Shh."

Drake watched the scene play out a moment. Nudged Rink with an elbow. Gestured for them to go to the hallway. Give the siblings a few minutes alone.

Lukas saw the movement. Stopped them before they got more than a step.

"How bad is it?"

No preamble. No lead-in.

Straight to business.

Drake glanced to Rink. Got a nod to go ahead.

"What do you remember?" Drake asked. Took a step into the room. Motioned for Rink to do the same.

Closed the door behind them.

They left the lights off. Didn't want to draw attention. Wanted to let Lukas wake up a bit more.

"Everything," Lukas whispered. Voice thick, moisture tugging at the underside of his eyes.

"Everything?" Rink asked. Instantly looked like he regretted saying the word.

It was out before he had a chance to stop it.

"Mhmm," Lukas grunted. Raised his chin in a bit of a nod. "Everything up until the paramedics lifted me into the squad. I willed myself to stay awake that long. You know, just in case."

The admission brought another surge of tears from Sara.

A flush of blood rushed to Drake's face. He could feel it warm beneath his skin. Tickling at the small of his back.

"How long have I been out?" Lukas asked. Looked to Sara, unable to speak. To Rink, staring at the floor.

Finally to Drake.

"Just over a week," Drake said. "You were hit three times, one of them to your lung. They kept you in a coma until your body was strong enough to breathe on its own."

Lukas nodded. Seemed to be adding things up in his head.

"You know I was in the service eight years? Eight years, and the worst thing that happened to me was a sprained knee. I get out and two weeks later I'm shot up and in a coma."

The thick sound in his voice faded, replaced by a touch of anger.

Bitterness.

Drake opened his mouth to speak. Closed it. Looked over to Sara.

She seemed to sense what he was getting at. Nodded for him to continue.

"Lukas, I'm about to throw a lot at you, and I need you to try your best to process all of it, okay?"

Lukas looked at him. Said nothing.

"My guess is you already know a fair bit of it, but I'm going to walk you through what we have anyway. I'm sorry to have to do this right now, but we don't have a lot of time."

The stare continued.

"Time before what?" Lukas asked.

"Before the Sheriff comes and places you under arrest," Drake replied.

If the information surprised Lukas, he didn't let it show. He stared back, unblinking.

"They're going to take me in like this?"

"No," Drake replied. "You'll stay here until well enough to move. Just the same, you will be considered under arrest. Guards will be posted outside your door.

"I will be the only person allowed to speak to you without supervision."

Lukas shot a glance to Sara.

"Let's hear it."

Drake walked to the foot of the bed. Drew over a stool. Lowered himself down onto it.

"The reason we asked for you to be woken up right now is you have information nobody else has. This might be the only chance we have to talk before you get taken into custody.

"And it could be the only way to keep you from going to jail for a very long time."

All three people stared back at Drake in silence.

"Now, in a couple of hours, the Sheriff is going to come and arrest you. There might be a press conference. I'm sure the County Attorney will try to get her face on TV. At the very least, her name in the paper.

"None of that matters. Not really, anyway. Like I said, you won't be going anywhere for a while."

Sara lowered her head at the mention of Lukas being arrested. Said nothing.

Drake drew in a deep breath. Debated his next words.

Looked back at the three darkened visages before him.

"When you were brought in here a week ago, Rink called and asked me to come speak with Sara. The Sheriff had already told her he was going to lock you up. The prosecuting attorney told the world she was going to push for the maximum penalty.

"Attempted murder. Life in prison."

The words drew a disgusted scowl from Lukas.

"Murder? What?"

Drake raised a hand. Nodded.

"I agree. I'll get to that. Sara asked me to look into things. See exactly why you did what you did.

"Here's the best of what I can tell. I'll run through it fast, then you fill in the holes. That work?"

Lukas waved a hand. "You have my attention."

Drake glanced to each of the others as well.

He had the whole room's attention.

"I started with your recent discharge. There was talk in the news of this being a recent serviceman getting out, having trouble adjusting to civilian life."

"Bullshit," Lukas spat.

Drake continued without pause.

"Rink here spoke to your friends with the Home Guard. They were able to get me in with Dr. Woodson over in Helena. Took her less than 20 minutes to tell me you were the least affected returning soldier she'd ever seen."

A bit of a crease appeared at the corner of Lukas's mouth.

"Nice lady. I liked her."

Drake nodded in agreement. "So I came back here, went to talk to the Home Guard. Asked them if there was any chance a man with your skills would walk into a meeting, start firing, and not hit a soul."

"Only if I didn't want to," Lukas said.

"That's exactly what they said," Drake replied. "So we figured you must have been trying to tell somebody something. Went to take a look at the Town Hall scene.

"That was some mighty impressive shooting."

Lukas snorted. "As big as his head is? I could have hit that with a pea shooter."

A small smirk escaped Drake's lips. "That's where we went next. And you're not wrong. Guy was a prick. Lied through his teeth to us."

"What did you ask him?" Lukas said.

"Nothing, really," Drake replied. "Which is why it was so odd that he lied about everything. Painted a bullseye on himself from that moment forward."

Lukas rolled his head to the side. Looked at his sister.

"He put that bullseye in place long before you met with him."

Again, Drake raised a hand. Wanted to get through his assessment.

"The next morning, I spoke to Wanda Pritchett. Learned two very important things. First was the bright red light."

"Tracers," Lukas mumbled.

Drake nodded. "Which I learned about a little later on my next trip out to see the Home Guard.

"The other thing I found out was I had a tail. Tierney was having me followed."

The skin around Lukas's eyes tightened. His jaw clenched.

"McIlvaine?"

"You know him?" Drake asked. Raised his eyebrows a bit up his forehead.

"I ought to," Lukas said. "Son of a bitch shot me."

"Three times," Rink added.

An angry breath passed through Lukas's nose. He shifted his attention back to Drake.

"I guess he first showed up a couple of months ago. About the time all this started. We'll get to that in a minute though. Go ahead."

Nodded for him to continue.

"Based on what Pritchett and the Guard told me, I followed a hunch. Went to the U and met with a guy, had him explain everything he knew to me about brucellosis."

At the mention of the word, Lukas reclined his head back a bit. Looked hard at Drake.

"Impressive," Lukas replied.

"So here's what I'm thinking," Drake said. Glanced again to Rink.

"Something's going on with Tierney and brucellosis. Maybe his herd has it. Maybe he's pushing hard for this new law change everybody's against. That part I need your help on.

"You showed up at the Agriculture Commission meeting to discuss it, but he shut you down. Wouldn't even let you speak.

"Once he did, you went outside and made sure they heard you."

Silence fell as Drake stopped talking. Rink and Sara both looked at him. Shifted their gaze to Lukas.

For a moment, all three sat looking at him, his features grim in the shadows of the room.

"Impressive," he said again. "But you missed you one thing. Tierney's herd doesn't have brucellosis.

"Ours does."

CHAPTER THIRTY-SEVEN

Silence.

Complete, pin-drop silence.

No breathing apparatus. No heartrate monitor.

The thought of breaking it entered Drake's mind, of asking exactly what Lukas meant. That, or any of the untold number of other questions shoving their way in right behind it.

He pushed them all to the side. Knew to wait it out. Lukas would get to his explanation when he was ready.

Sara wasn't quite so patient.

"What do you mean *we* have brucellosis?" Sara asked. "How do you know this? Why didn't you say anything?"

Lukas rolled his head to the side. Looked at her.

"I just found out a couple weeks ago myself. Papa told me. Asked me not to say anything."

"Not to say anything?" Sara asked. Her voice higher. Hurt, frustration both mixed in. "How can he ask that? How can you do that?"

"I'm sorry, I was just-"

"When will either of you start treating me like an equal part in this business?"

Rink pressed his lips tight. Turned his head at the neck to glance at Drake.

Drake matched the look. Gave no outward reaction at all.

"You're right," Lukas said. Reached down and squeezed Sara's hand. "You need to hear this."

Turned so he faced forward. Could see both Rink and Drake in his field of vision.

"All of you."

He paused a moment. Closed his eyes. Swallowed hard.

"For about the last 10 years, the ranch has been getting squeezed. Rising oil costs. New rates on state leases for pasture lands. Grain and feed going through the roof.

"At the same time, beef prices have stayed about the same. No drop-off to speak of, but definitely not keeping up with inflation."

Drake leaned forward. Rested his elbows on his knees.

Waited.

"Tierney first started coming around about five years ago. Our ranches touch up on the back-end, and he was looking to expand his operation. With over 5,000 head, they were eating their way through every bit of grass he had."

Sara's jaw dropped. Her face fell flat.

"Papa was talking about selling?"

"No," Lukas said. Shook his head. "The first time he came around, Papa politely declined. Tierney knew we were getting pinched though and kept coming around, kept dropping his offer price.

"By the fourth or fifth time, the two descended into open hostility. Papa told him to go to Hell and never come back."

"I had no idea," Sara said. "When was this?"

"The last time was about three months ago," Lukas said. "Less than a week before our first cow tested positive for brucellosis. Just a random spot check, and there it was."

A flag went off in the back of Drake's mind. He recalled the words of Riley. Played them off of what Lukas was saying now.

Something didn't add up.

"I thought in Tier Two, testing was only done when taking an animal to slaughter?" Drake asked.

Lukas shifted his gaze to Drake and nodded. "You've done your homework. Yeah, that's right, or at least it's supposed to be.

"Right before that, the local Ag Commission decided to start doing random pop-up tests in the area. Said it was to protect everybody."

Drake leaned back. Lifted his chin toward the ceiling.

"So Tierney uses his position on the board to put this new policy in effect, then gives your dad one last chance to sell him the land."

"And when he says no, you guys get tested," Rink finished. Glanced from Drake to Lukas.

Drake nodded. "Still though - and no offense - but sham of a policy or not, your cow still tested positive."

"That's just it," Lukas said. "I said our *herd* tested positive, not our *cows*."

Sara's brow furrowed. "Difference being?"

"Difference being, the two cows that tested positive weren't our cows. They were his."

The information brought Drake to his feet. He ran a hand back over his scalp. Paced the width of the room.

Beside him, Rink folded and refolded his arms.

"But, that doesn't make any sense," Drake said. "How-"

"If you know about the tiers in the state," Lukas said. "You also know that once an animal in a herd tests positive – any animal – the entire bunch is under quarantine. Tierney knew we wouldn't be able to survive that and the additional cost of testing every animal."

"So all he had to do was get you guys to have a single positive test and you were sunk," Drake said. Continued pacing.

"Yup," Lukas said. His face fell flat as he stared down at the thin white blanket stretched across him.

"It was the last conversation my father and I ever had. When we should have been saying goodbye, he was explaining to me how to save the ranch."

His eyes went glassy as he shifted his attention to Sara.

"Please, don't be angry. It's how he wanted it. He was old school, you know that. You were his little girl. He couldn't stand the idea of mixing you up in it."

Matching tears raced down either of Sara's cheeks. She said nothing.

"But," Drake said. Still pacing. One hand in his pocket. The other scratching the back of his head. "How do you know they were his cows?"

Lukas turned his attention back to Drake. Gave a wan smile.

"The brands. After they tested positive, the animals were destroyed, but all identifying marks were photographed for record keeping purposes.

"After Papa's funeral, I filed a formal appeal. Asked to have copies of those photos sent to the house."

Sara's eyes grew wide. She rose up several inches in her seat. Stared from Lukas to Drake and back again.

"Is that why you were watching the mail like a hawk? I thought you were waiting on something from the Army."

"No," Lukas said. "I was waiting on those copies. The minute I saw them, I knew what had happened.

"The son of a bitch rebranded his cows to match ours."

CHAPTER THIRTY-EIGHT

Spit-shined.

Everything about Sheriff Jacob Pratt was polished to a gleam.

The nameplate on his uniform. His belt buckle. The clasp on his hatband. Even his shoes, for the first time since leaving the store.

Everything.

There was a little extra bounce in his step as he pulled his cruiser to a stop in front of Hamilton Memorial. Ignored the posted handicapped placard. Parked front and center.

If there ended up being a press conference - and he had a feeling there would be - he wanted as many reminders of his presence visible as possible.

This was his moment. The time to prove to voters what kind of man they put their trust in.

Who they could fall asleep at night knowing watched over them.

Two deputies waited for him by the front door as he entered. Young pups. Walsh and LeGrange. Neither a day over 24.

Both brimming with excitement, unable to stand still.

Pratt looked at both of them. Barely able to contain the pride he felt.

Offered a controlled smile.

"Morning, boys."

"Boss," LeGrange mumbled.

"Sir," Walsh added.

Without breaking stride, Pratt led them toward Webb's room. Let them fan out to either side. Stayed a step ahead.

Marched through the halls in a flying V formation. The fabled spearhead of justice coming to do its job.

Butterflies kicked up in his stomach as he rounded the last corner. Heat flushed his face. Brought sweat to his brow. Upper lip. Lower back.

Something felt off the moment he came into view of his destination.

There were no doctors moving about. No nurses rushing to and fro. No medical personnel of any kind visible.

Nothing more than Kellogg, half-asleep, leaning against the window sill. Staring out at another grey morning.

Across from him, Webb's door stood closed.

The look of pride fled from Pratt's face. Butterflies turned to dread.

He was half-afraid to ask the question, but forced himself to anyway.

"What's going on?"

Kellogg snapped alert at the sound of his voice. Turned. Looked sheepish that he'd been caught dozing.

"They're still in there."

"Still?" Pratt asked. "How long does it take to wake someone up?"

The color drained from Kellogg's face. He opened his mouth to speak, but no words came out.

The sense of dread swelled within Pratt. Landed in his stomach with a sickening thud.

"What?"

"They woke him up last night," Kellogg said.

Pratt's shoulders drooped. His eyes bulged.

"You're shitting me. Then who's he in there with?"

"His family," Kellogg said. Looked away. "His lawyer."

The shock of just a moment before subsided. Anger flooded in behind it. Pratt's face got red. His chest swelled.

"You have *got* to be shitting me!"

Pratt left Kellogg standing slack-jawed in the hallway. Stomped his way for the door beside him.

Banged on it with the ball of his fist.

"This is Sheriff Jacob Pratt, I'm coming in."

Before his hand reached the handle, the door swung open from within.

On the bed sat Lukas Webb, very much awake and alert. Beside him was his sister, the girl Pratt spoke with a week before.

Around them were two guys in their mid-20s Pratt had never seen. He did a quick assessment and figured the one with blonde hair to be the lawyer.

None of the four looked surprised by his entrance.

"Lukas Webb, I am here to place you under arrest for the shooting that occurred on December 22nd at the Hamilton Town Hall.

"You have the right to remain silent. Anything you say can and will be used against you in a court of law. You have the right to an attorney. If you cannot afford one, one will be appointed for you. Do you understand these rights as I have read them to you?"

The slightest of a smirk lifted Webb's head back an inch. He glanced over to the blonde guy.

"He knows you're standing here, right?"

Pratt felt another flush of heat beneath his skin.

"Yeah, but he has to say it," the blonde replied. "We can get the whole thing tossed if he doesn't Mirandize you."

"Ah," Lukas said. Tilted his head back in understanding. "So, we're good here?"

At those words, Sara and the other young man both rose. Walked from the room. Didn't look at Pratt or his deputies.

The blonde lingered a moment longer. Glanced to Pratt. Nodded.

"Remember what we talked about. We'll see you soon."

The blonde exited. Nodded to each of the deputies as he went.

Pratt turned and watched him go. Leveled his gaze on Webb. Stood there for a full moment.

"Obviously, we can't move you right now, but you are hereby placed into custody. My men will be here around the clock from now on and will supervise all visits until you are physically able to be moved."

Webb nodded.

"I understand."

Pratt hooked his thumbs in his belt. Shook his head. Muttered under his breath. Turned to Walsh.

"You boys stay in position here."

Walsh pressed his lips together. Nodded.

"Where are you headed, sir?"

The words barely reached Pratt's ears. He was already headed for the door.

"I've got to make a phone call. And she's not going to be happy."

CHAPTER THIRTY-NINE

Ten after 9:00.

Almost a full hour before she expected to arrive.

Even despite a bevy of last-second phone calls, a good 10 minutes before any media from Missoula would be on hand.

Paula Goslin slid her Chevy Silverado into the Memorial parking lot. Saw Pratt's cruiser parked front and center.

Scoffed.

She gave her hair one last check in the rearview mirror. Saw a mess of grey curls that hadn't been ready to come out of their rollers.

Scoffed again.

Taking up a leather briefcase from the seat beside her, she stepped out of the truck. Let the bag swing free by her side.

There was nothing in it. It was just a prop for the morning ahead. People expected to see a briefcase when they saw a lawyer interviewed on television.

At the moment, Goslin thought she might use it to hit Pratt upside the head.

Nostrils flared as she walked toward the front door. Saw Pratt step out to meet her, hands already raised in front of him.

Felt the same anger as when he'd first called well within her.

"How the hell could you let this happen?" she spat. Kept her voice low. Spoke through her teeth. Squeezed the handle of the briefcase in her hand.

"He's new," Pratt said. Shook his head. "He had explicit directions to call if anything changed, but I guess he got confused."

"Confused? You asked him to pick up the phone and make a call, not perform Chinese algebra!"

Pratt looked away. Sighed.

"I know. I know. But the important thing is, Lukas Webb is now awake and in our custody."

Goslin turned away from Pratt. Muttered under her breath.

She wasn't surprised that he was shifting the blame onto some nameless kid with a badge. He'd been doing that the entirety of the 20 years they'd worked together.

This was just the first time his incompetence had negatively impacted her chance at recognition.

"No thanks to you," Goslin said. Turned to see a van from KMSL News pull into the lot. "Good thing the kid just got out of a coma, or he'd be halfway to Mexico by now."

The remark found its target. Dropped Pratt's jaw toward the ground.

Goslin left him gaping outside the front door. Met the KMSL van by the curb.

From it emerged two people, neither much older than 20. Out of the front seat climbed a girl with too-blonde hair. Too-white teeth. A stylish coat and scarf combo.

Stumbling from the back was a guy with curly hair. Patchy beard. Net trucker's cap turned backwards. Puffy vest and jeans.

Smelled fresh off an all-night bender.

Behind the wheel sat a slovenly man who made no attempt to climb out.

It took an extreme amount of effort for Goslin not to roll her eyes at the scene.

She had requested media on hand to cover a very important arrest, not to send the local high school's A/V department.

"Good morning," the girl said. Stuck her hand out. "I'm Kelli Morris and this is my cameraman Beau Axle."

Axle stopped moving for a moment. Thrust his chin upward in greeting.

Goslin returned the handshake. "Charmed. Thank you for coming."

Made sure her tone relayed that they were not who she was expecting to see.

It went right past Morris.

"Okay," Kelli said. "So while Beau gets us up and ready, is there anywhere in particular that you'd like to do this?"

A heavy sigh rolled out of Goslin. She turned over her shoulder. Glanced at the sign welcoming visitors to the Hamilton Memorial Hospital.

"We can do it right here, if you'd like. Get the sign in the background."

The morning was already turning into a disaster. Might as well add a bout of hypothermia to it.

"Perfect," Kelli said. Returned to the van and extracted her microphone as Axel rummaged through the back.

Goslin stepped away for a moment. Debated going inside to wait. Opted against it so as to not be flushed bright red from returning to the cold.

Off to the side, she could see Pratt lingering. Made a point to avoid eye contact. Not to go anywhere near him.

Let body language relay her ongoing disgust with his handling of the situation.

Ten minutes after arriving, Axel positioned Morris and Goslin under the sign. Hefted the camera to his shoulder. Counted backwards from three.

Goslin took a deep breath as he did so. Waited for the red light.

Put on her best grim face as it blinked to life.

Beside her, Morris was nothing but smiles. A ray of sunshine on a grey Montana morning.

It almost made Goslin sick.

"Good morning, this is Kelli Morris reporting on-site at Hamilton Memorial Hospital for KMSL News. With me is Ravalli County Attorney Paula Goslin to announce that a week after the horrific shooting that took place at a local Agriculture Commission meeting, an arrest has been made."

Morris thrust the microphone over.

Goslin felt her eyebrows rise. It was a better lead-in than she expected.

"That is correct, Kelli. As of 8:00 this morning, Lukas Webb, the man that opened fire on a peaceably assembled civic meeting last week, has been placed under arrest."

Morris pulled the microphone back.

"And just to remind viewers, this was a bit of an unusual situation that called for such a delay, correct?"

"It was," Goslin said. Nodded. "A local man with a concealed carry permit returned fire on Webb, striking him three times. His combined injuries led doctors to place him in a medically-induced coma.

"This morning, a reversing agent was applied and upon his waking, the arrest was made."

Morris looked right at her with a look of faux concern.

"This is a big win for the people of Hamilton," Goslin continued. "Even though we have been monitoring Webb all week, it is important for them to see that he has been formally apprehended. Justice is and will be served."

Goslin look right into the camera as she spoke. Used the tone reserved for courtroom theatrics.

"You mentioned a few days ago that the state will be pursuing maximum charges for this offense," Morris said. "Is this still your intention?"

"Absolutely," Goslin said. "This was not a mere instance of someone discharging a weapon in a public place. Lukas Webb left the meeting, went to his truck and obtained a high-powered rifle, returned and began shooting.

"This was nothing short of attempted murder, and I intend to prosecute it that way."

Morris nodded. Pulled the microphone back away from Goslin once more.

"I understand Mr. Webb was a returning veteran," she said. "Is this true?"

Goslin pressed her lips together. It was a question she didn't really want to answer. Had prepared for just in case.

"It is true, and it speaks to a much larger issue in our society today. We must commit to take better care of our discharged veterans. We have to ensure their physical and mental well-being so they are not a danger to themselves or others once they return."

One final time Morris pulled the microphone back. Stared into the camera.

"Reporting from Hamilton, this is Kelli Morris, KMSL News."

Axel paused a moment. The red light blinked out. He lowered the camera away from his head.

"Looked good. Thanks a lot," he said. Voice much higher than expected.

"Thank you so much," Morris said. Pushed the microphone into her left hand. Thrust out her right.

Goslin accepted it. Gave a stiff handshake.

Nothing about the morning had played out the way it was supposed to. Now it just needed to be over.

"My pleasure, thank you for being here."

Less than 20 minutes after arriving, the news crew waved goodbye. Goslin stood in place and watched as they left the parking lot.

In their wake, for the first time noticed Drake Bell standing by his truck, listening to every word.

CHAPTER FORTY

WB.

Two letters side-by-side.

The brand of the Webb Ranch.

Constructed from bent Rebar, it hung down from the gate across their driveway. Passed less than two feet above the cab of Drake's truck.

Swayed back and forth in the wind.

Gravel crunched beneath his tires as he pulled in and came to a stop beside Rink's rig. Climbed out and headed inside.

Even though he'd never been there before, the place wasn't hard to find. Most of the roads in Hamilton were laid out in a basic grid.

The entirety of Sara's direction to him were "third light, make a right. Two point eight miles out on your left."

To his surprise, it really was that simple.

True to the descriptions given by both Sara and Lukas, the WB Ranch was a far cry from the Tierney spread.

A modest house sat at the end of a gravel lane. Single story. Ranch style. Brick halfway up. White siding the rest of the way.

A small handful of barns sat out back. Painted red. White trim.

A mid-sized cluster of cows milled about one of them. A pair of tractors were parked by another.

Everything was clean, but lifeless.

Drake knocked on the front door. Let himself into a screened-in porch. Knocked a second time on an inner door.

Heard Sara call from within to enter.

Turning the door knob, he stepped inside to find the home small. Cozy. A bit outdated.

The furniture was sturdy. Covered in fabric with patterned designs. Spots worn down from repeated use.

Brown loop carpeting covered the floors. Made the entire place seem a little darker.

A potbelly stove stood silent in the corner.

Drake followed the sound of papers rustling through the living room. Found Rink and Sara on either side of a cherry dining room table. Each had a stack of pages in hand.

A pair of printouts were set aside.

"How'd it go?" Sara asked. Looked up from the documents she held.

"About like you'd expect. This is a big win for justice, the people of Hamilton can now sleep easy at night, all that crap."

Sara rolled her eyes. Went back to her work.

"You're going to make her eat those words, right?" Rink asked. Didn't look up from what he was doing.

"Oh, yeah," Drake said. Let the corner of his mouth play up into a smile. "The last thing she did was go on this tangent about how we need to do a better job caring for our returning veterans. I'm going to have a lot of fun with that one."

Rink nodded. "Good."

Drake twisted his neck to the side. Looked down at the pair of print-outs on the table.

Picked them up and studied them close.

"You found them."

Neither person answered as he stared down at the papers. Full color copies of original photographs.

Both were close-up shots of a cattle brand.

Both resembled the WB Drake had driven under a moment before, but just barely.

"What's Tierney's brand again?" Drake asked. Tried to decipher what the original symbols might have been.

Sara put down the stack she was looking at. Moved to Drake's shoulder. "TR, for Tierney Ranch."

"Original."

"Right?" Sara asked. Outlined with her finger what the initial brand had looked like. How it had been doctored to resemble theirs.

Drake followed her finger, picking out the first brand.

"I'll be damned," he muttered. Stared at the new design.

To someone that might not know better, the brand resembled what it was supposed to.

Once the forgery was pointed out though, it was impossible to ignore.

"This is good," Drake said.

"Yeah?" Sara asked. "Everything we need?"

Drake pulled the photographs away from his face. Raised his gaze. "Yes and no. These copies won't get us anywhere. Just looking at them you can tell the brand's been messed with. There's no way the Sheriff would believe we didn't do this ourselves."

A stack of papers slapped against the table. Rink sidled up on the opposite of Drake. Studied the pictures.

"You're right. Those look like bad Photoshop pictures."

"Mhmm," Drake agreed.

"You said yes and no," Sara said.

"Right," Drake said. "The only way photographs ever get admitted as evidence is through a chain of custody. An official record of certified personnel handing them off one to another.

"These pictures came from the State Department of Ag. We can get them to show the originals to the Sheriff."

"Okay, so let's do that," Sara said.

Drake shook his head. "There's the problem. This is Saturday and Monday's a holiday. The first chance we'd have is Tuesday."

Rink shook his head. Stepped away. Picked up the stack of papers again.

"At least he's in the hospital and not actual jail?" Sara said. A small crack in her voice. Tears not far off.

Drake barely heard either.

His attention was focused on the barn outside. On the cluster of cows huddling behind it.

"Unless..." he whispered. Let his voice trail off.

Sara and Rink both looked at him. Remained silent.

Rink turned at the waist. Followed Drake's sightline out the window. Back again.

"Unless what?"

Drake blinked twice. Flicked his gaze over to Rink.

"Lukas said the two cows that tested positive did so at a spot-check. What if there are more out there that haven't been found yet?"

Rink turned all the way around. Stared at the cows standing in place.

"Sara, how many head do you have here?"

"This time of year?" Sara said. "I don't know exactly. Maybe just shy of 1,000?"

She glanced from Drake to Rink and back again.

"You think?"

"No way to argue the authenticity of a living, breathing cow," Drake said. "We find one, we can load it up and take it right to the Sheriff. Even call up their friends at KMSL if we have to."

A snort rolled out of Rink.

"I like it. Sonsabitches."

Sara's mouth hung open. A look of worry crossed her face.

"I do too, but like I said, there are over 1,000 cows out there, and only three of us."

Drake smiled. Pulled his phone from his pocket.

"True, but I know how we can have three more here in less than an hour."

CHAPTER FORTY-ONE

Paused.

Holt froze the screen in place.

Left the image of Paula Goslin standing with her mouth half-open on the television. Made sure the banner across the bottom could be seen.

White letters on a blue background.

Lukas Webb Arrested.

Holt waited several seconds. Swiveled his chair to face forward. Leveled an accusatory gaze on McIlvaine across from him.

"Care to explain?"

McIlvaine looked bored. Disgusted. Glanced to the screen. Back to Holt.

His entire attitude burned Holt to no end. Made him want to grab the nickel-plated Colt he kept in his desk drawer.

Do to McIlvaine what he'd done to Webb.

Only difference being he would finish the job.

Still, for as much as he was fast coming to loathe the man, to regret hiring him in the first place, he still needed him.

A little longer yet, anyway.

"Nothing to explain," McIlvaine said. "I got in unnoticed, but his sister showed up before I could do anything."

Anger flashed behind Holt's eyes. Rose in the back of his throat.

"So you just left?"

"Seemed smarter than getting caught committing murder, don't you think?"

Holt snorted. "So you mean to tell me you did manage to think while acting this time?"

McIlvaine scowled across the desk. Holt could tell he wanted to lash out at him. Had been dying to since he showed up with lights and music blaring a couple nights ago.

To Holt's surprise, he held his tongue.

Both sides knew it was a partnership fast coming to a close. Best to just finish what needed to be done and get out before things got any messier.

"Look," McIlvaine said. "I tried. But it's not like this guy was out riding a trail somewhere or something. He was strapped down in a bed in the middle of a hospital.

"Mirrors, cameras, security lights."

Alarm bells went off in Holt's brain. He'd assumed that self-preservation alone would induce McIlvaine to be careful. Remain unseen. Move out of sight.

Any assumption where McIlvaine was concerned was fast looking like a poor one.

"Were you seen?" Holt asked.

"If I was seen, I'd be crossing the border into Canada by now," McIlvaine replied. Let ice hang from his tone.

Made no effort to hide the challenge in his eyes.

Holt met the gaze. Matched the animosity behind it.

"What's done, or in this case *isn't* done, is done. Let's figure out how we can end this now."

McIlvaine stared back at him. Said nothing.

"When Lukas showed up that night, I thought it was because he was pissed about the positive tests in his herd. Wanted to get our support to challenge the quarantine period and the mandatory testing for his whole operation."

Again, silence was the only response.

"In thinking about it though, I'm thinking that maybe somehow he saw the brands."

McIlvaine's eyes narrowed a bit. He said nothing.

Holt studied him.

"Be honest. How obvious is the re-brand?"

The stare remained a moment. Was broken by a snort. Deep. Derisive. It lifted McIlvaine's entire head by a couple of inches.

"You serious? It's a rebrand. Trying to take a charred piece of cow's ass and make it look like something else."

Holt's eyes grew hard. His jaw clenched.

"How? Obvious?"

McIlvaine made a show of rolling his eyes. Waving his hands by his side.

"Pretty damn. I mean, you can't tell if you're just walking by, but if you stop and look, yeah. You can see it. There aren't many ways to make a TR look like a WB you know."

Lightning flashed behind Holt's eyes. He pressed forward. Leaned his elbows on the desk.

"I thought you made a new brand?"

McIlvaine matched the pose.

"I did, but that doesn't get rid of the old brand. Burning something new doesn't just eliminate the original."

Holt turned his head to the side. Drew in a long breath.

Pushed out it slow and even through his mouth.

"That's what I was afraid of."

McIlvaine paused a moment. Leaned back in his chair. Crossed his legs. Rested an elbow on his knee.

"Yeah? What's that?"

"We have to go get that last cow," Holt said. Shifted his gaze back to McIlvaine.

A blank look stared back at him.

Remained that way for several moments.

Didn't shift until a low chuckle rolled out of McIlvaine. Started deep in his abdomen. Grew louder. Soon shook his entire body as he threw his head back.

Laughed with gusto.

Remained that way for the better part of two minutes. Ignored the angry stare of Holt across from him.

"You old fool, you're crazier than I thought."

Holt pressed his lips together. Felt venom rise through his body. Begin to seep from his pores.

Again fought the urge to reach for his gun.

"You remember where you are and who you're talking to."

"I should say the same to you," McIlvaine spat back. "You've been sending me on fool's errands all week, and now you expect me to go find one cow in a field of thousands?

"Then what? Get rid of it like the others?"

Holt seethed. Willed himself to calm down. Not to let Bernice hear him yelling in the next room.

"We are in this together."

"Ha!" McIlvaine said. Voice so loud it was almost a shout. "We're not in anything together. I've been a hired hand from the word go."

"Exactly," Holt said. "And that makes us partners. Maybe not equal partners, but partners just the same."

McIlvaine leaned forward. Twisted his head. Squinted his eyes.

"I hate to break it to you old man, but there isn't a single thing here anybody can pin on me. Moving cows, changing brands, hiding positive tests, it's all your ranch. Every last thing goes back to you, not me."

Heat rushed to Holt's face. The air slid from his lungs. He tried to form the words to fire back. To verbalize the contempt within him.

All he managed was, "Why, I ought to..."

"Yeah, but you won't," McIlvaine said. Gave him a dismissive wave of the hand.

Holt leaned back in his chair. Added up everything McIlvaine was telling him.

Realized he was absolutely right.

Panic flooded into his mind. His heartbeat raced. Air refused to enter his lungs.

For a moment, he felt like a heart attack was just a moment away.

Not until a single thought entered his brain did the anxiety subside.

Cold sweat drenched his face as he glanced up. Hated the taste of the words before he even asked them.

Still, it was the only way.

It was what had brought on this mess in the first place. It was the only thing that would end it.

"How much would it cost for you to go finish this thing tonight?"

CHAPTER FORTY-TWO

Threes.

Two groups of three, headed in opposite directions.

Sara, Rink, Ajax. Start next to the house. Work through the cows hugging the barn. Move their way back as they go.

Drake, Sage, Kade. Go to the far corner of the Webb land. Head toward the middle.

There wasn't enough time to get out the horses. Too cold to bother with trying to get the four-wheelers started.

Instead, everybody bundled into their Arctic gear. The first group set out from the house on foot.

Drake drove the others around the long way to the back field gate. Parked. Climbed out.

Each side took one copy of the picture. Studied it.

Moved out as fast they could.

The trio sat three across in the front of Drake's truck as he drove. Fought the natural inclination to turn the heat up high.

Kept it warm, but not hot. Didn't want the temperature swing when they stepped outside to be too jolting.

"Long night there, Bags?" Sage asked from the middle. Glanced over to Drake's profile beside her.

"I think it still qualifies as one long day at this point," Drake said. Checked in the rearview mirror. Saw that Sage was not wrong.

Dark circles belied his eyes. Hung in wide crescents.

"Which day?" Kade asked.

"Exactly," Drake said. Turned the truck off the main road. Bounced along a two-track toward the barn standing in the distance.

Heard the sound of tall grasses slapping at the undercarriage beneath them.

Drake lowered his head a bit. Peered up at the sky overhead. Glanced at the clock on the dash.

"Figure we've got, what? Maybe an hour of daylight left?"

Kade grunted in response.

"If that," Sage said. Pulled her ski gloves on.

"Thank you guys again for doing this," Drake said. Watched as the barn drew closer.

"Don't do that," Sage said. "That's not how this works."

"Besides, I don't even know if it's you that should be thanking us," Kade added.

Drake considered the statement. Smirked.

Best he could figure, it was a favor to him, Rink, and Sara all three.

The barn was little more than a lean-to. Two adjacent sides to form a corner constructed from concrete block. A simple flat shingled roof overhead.

Drake pulled the truck up alongside it. Killed the engine. Smashed a hat down over his head and climbed out.

Went to the chrome toolbox stretched the width of his truck bed. Opened and extracted a pair of flashlights. Extended one each to Sage and Kade.

"In case you need them."

They both accepted the implements without comment.

"You guys good on the brand?"

"Find the one that looks like a really bad tattoo?" Kade asked.

"Yes," Drake replied. "Find the one that resembles what some poor girl that woke up with your name on her arm did to try and alter it."

Sage cracked a smile as the three headed into the barn. Did a quick pass through. Checked over no more than two dozen cows.

Found nothing close to what they were looking for.

After the last one, Drake walked out from beneath the roof. Surveyed the land around them.

There was no way to get the truck inside the fence line. No major choke points anywhere visible.

"Alright," he said. "Let's fan out. Stay in sight of one another. Move fast."

Face determined, Kade nodded. Took off at a jog.

Sage reached out. Ran a hand down Drake's arm. Brought her lips together in a tight smile.

Moved out straight ahead.

Drake watched her go. Looped around to the right. Tucked in close to the fence and started moving inward.

Overhead, the sky continued to darken. The thick cloud cover blocked most of the sunlight from view. Brought nightfall even earlier than expected.

Dropped the temperature with each passing minute.

Drake's breathing filled his ears as he jogged from one clump of cattle to the next. The animals, content and docile, barely looked at him as he checked them over.

Saw nothing out of the ordinary.

Moved on.

As he went, the animals remained huddled close together. Served as wind blocks for one another. Chewed the few tufts of grass that weren't frozen stiff.

A sheen of sweat formed along Drake's torso as he ran. The smell of animal fur and hay filled his nostrils.

For the briefest of moments, he allowed himself to think how under different circumstances the experiences might be peaceful. Perhaps even cathartic.

The moment passed as he saw Sage's flashlight kick on in the distance. Kade's right after it.

The barn and his truck fell from view as they continued moving. Tracked down more cattle.

Saw nothing close to what they were looking for.

A shrill whistle went up nearby. Drew Drake's attention over to Kade, who stood with an arm outstretched.

Drake followed his index finger out in a straight line. Saw what Kade was pointing to.

A second outpost barn, its silhouette visible against the darkening sky.

Drake circled a hand over his head in recognition. Doubled his pace. Moved just slow enough to keep from spooking the cows.

By the time he reached the barn, Sage was already there. She stood with her back to him, hands resting atop her head. No doubt panting from her run as well.

Kade was moving fast. A little over 50 yards out and closing.

Sweat poured down Drake's face. The cold air tore at his lungs as he approached.

Panting, he rested his hands on his hips. Walked up slow, the interior of the barn dark.

"You find anything?" he asked.

The sound of a gun cocking rang out. Stopped Drake where he stood. Sent his heart pounding even harder than before.

"Oh yeah, she found something, alright," a voice said. Not quite familiar, but recognizable.

Drake stood rooted in place. Tried to place it.

Watched as Hank McIlvaine emerged from the shadows.

CHAPTER FORTY-THREE

Click.

The unmistakable sound of the hammer on a gun being drawn back. Ready to drop down. Smash the firing pin.

Spit hot metal into the night.

Drake's breath caught in his throat as he stood. Raised his hands out to the side. Stepped close enough to let his fingertips graze Sage's arm.

Felt her body rigid beneath his touch.

"Yeah, I know you're out there, too," McIlvaine called. Stared out into the gathering darkness. "I'll never find you in the dark, but I don't have."

He smiled. Extended the gun out in front of him.

"You have 10 seconds to show yourself before I start shooting."

Drake kept his gaze on McIlvaine. Didn't bother to look over and see if Kade would show.

There was no way he'd risk getting him and Sage hurt.

He would be there. And he wouldn't be happy about it.

It took just over six seconds, Drake counting them off slow in his head, before Kade could be heard crunching through the darkness. Showed himself on the opposite side of Sage.

Stayed several feet away.

Drake cast one quick glance. Saw the scowl on Kade's face.

Knew he was staying out of reach in case McIlvaine got jumpy with his trigger finger. More targets. Further apart.

For a moment, he considered trying to do the same. Cast the idea aside.

He needed to be close enough to try and shield Sage if things went down.

"Well then," McIlvaine said. Kept the same cocksure smile in place. "Now that we've got that taken care of."

He switched the gun into his left hand. Kept it extended in front of him. Unsnapped a lead rope from his hip.

Alternated glances between the group and a cow tucked against the side of the barn.

Solid black. A single splotch of white on her rear hip.

In the darkness she looked like little more than a shadow. The only thing that gave her presence away was the shine of her eyes. The sound of her chewing a mouthful of alfalfa.

If the appearance of four people troubled her at all, there was no sign of it.

Drake watched as McIlvaine shuffled two steps to the side. Lifted the rope over the cow's head. Closed it with a slip knot.

Gaze fixed on the group, he pulled her over to the side. Had to lean into it at first to get her going. Pulled himself upright as she reluctantly followed his lead.

"It would appear you guys are in luck," McIlvaine said. "I was paid a rather hefty sum to get rid of this here cow, but I have no reason to be shooting the three of you.

"Stay right where you are and this will be the last you ever see of me in these parts."

He took two more steps away from them. Stopped. Allowed the cow to come to a stop by his side.

"Actually, you know what? I like it here. I'm already getting rid of this thing, what's a few more bodies on the pile?"

Raised the gun. Smiled.

Drake nudged closer to Sage. Wrapped his fingers around the tail of her coat. Prepared to fling her backwards to the ground.

Felt his heart, his breath, stop in his chest.

Heard the sound of a gun rack.

Not McIlvaine's gun. Not the simple click of a hammer being pulled back and locked into place.

The heavy slide action of a rifle.

Drake was beyond being surprised. Long past feeling any additional burst of shock or fear.

Instead, he felt confusion. Squinted into the darkness. Tried to find the source of the noise.

Heard an identical sound come in from the opposite side. Shifted his attention to McIlvaine.

Saw the look of panic on his face. The mixture of trepidation and realization splayed across his features.

"I couldn't agree more," Jensen Hall said from the darkness. Walked up behind McIlvaine. Thrust one foot out in front of the other. Nice and easy. "What is one more body on the pile?"

To either side, the brothers that had been posted up at the bar emerged from the darkness. Dressed in black. Greased faces.

Assault rifles at the ready.

Between them, Hall was dressed the same. No face paint. No weapon.

McIlvaine's mouth and eyes formed three perfect circles. The color drained from his face.

Drake watched as he glanced over his shoulder at the men behind him. Turned as if he might open fire on the targets in front.

Hall seemed to sense what he was planning. Shook his head to the side.

"You even think about it, we will saw you in two before your finger squeezes."

The brothers converged on either side. Hub tore the gun from McIlvaine's hand. Shoved it down the back of his waistband.

His counterpart grabbed McIlvaine by the wrist. Wrapped a set of zip-tie cuffs around it. Cinched them tight.

For his part, McIlvaine put up no fight.

Any resolve he'd displayed over the last week was gone. In its place was pure, unadulterated fear. His gaze hung toward the ground. His arms went limp and lifeless.

One minute, he was threatening to murder three people in cold blood. The next, he was being led off into the darkness.

Drake had no doubt that his earlier words would be true.

None of them would ever see him again.

Drake took a half-step forward. Released his grip on Sage's coat. Spread his hand wide and rubbed her back.

"It's okay," he said. Felt Kade press in on the opposite side.

Hall waited until the brothers had McIlvaine far behind him. Took two steps forward into the barn and stared at Drake.

"I told you he wouldn't even know we were there."

"We didn't either," Drake said.

"You still don't," Hall said. Nodded once for emphasis.

Drake looked over Sage's head to Kade. Met his gaze. Shared a nod.

"Understood."

"What the hell are you guys doing out here anyway?" Hall asked. Folded his arms across his chest.

Drake motioned with his chin toward the cow. Standing exactly where McIlvaine had left her, lead rope still hanging down. "Her."

Hall smirked. Turned back in the direction he had come from.

"There are easier ways to get a burger you know."

Drake opened his mouth to respond. Stopped. Smiled. Watched as Hall retreated into the darkness.

"Thank you!" he called out.

Heard Hall's pace slow.

"You're welcome," Hall replied. "And keep doing what you're doing for Lukas. We appreciate it."

Drake waved a hand in affirmation. Said nothing.

"Oh," Hall said. Voice already growing further away. "And I trust you'll find some way to make Paula Goslin pay for that little speech she gave this morning too, huh?"

An involuntary smile spread across Drake's face.

"Be my pleasure, General."

CHAPTER FORTY-FOUR

Slow.

Painfully, excruciatingly slow.

And cold.

Bone chilling, frozen solid, cold.

Those were the only two words that came to mind as Drake hand-led a cow across a windswept patch of open pasture. Inch-by-inch over uneven ground. Stopping every 50 yards to let her grab up another bite of grass.

The first 100 yards, Kade and Sage fell in beside him. Walked along at an agonizing pace.

After that, Drake sent them on to the truck. Told them to call ahead and have Sara, Rink, and Ajax meet them.

To have the Sheriff waiting there, too.

They put up only a token defense, at best. Left Drake one of the flashlights. Took off at a brisk jog across the field.

Drake watched until the last beam of the other light disappeared into the darkness. Went back to tugging on the cow.

For the first time in two days, Drake was left to his thoughts. Alone to think about the last week.

Of how violently Lukas Webb's life had swung like a pendulum. Of the people he'd never met a few days ago.

The side of Rink he didn't know existed.

How long it had been since he'd slept.

With each step, the cold sapped a bit more of his strength. Pushed down on his eyelids.

"Come on girl," Drake said. Flexed some feeling back into fingers. Reached over and dug his hand into the skin folds between her ears.

In the darkness, he could see the moist disc of her eye roll over to look at him. By daylight, the eye would be warm Chesnutt brown.

Now, nothing but inky black, deep and serene, staring back at him.

A beef eater his entire life, it was the first time he'd ever been face to face with a cow. There was something peaceful about walking along beside her. Drinking in her calm demeanor.

Deep inside, some small part of him got a little sad. Not for the species as a whole. He was old enough, wise enough, to know how things worked.

He didn't like for anything to ever be killed. Understood the necessity of it, though.

In this instant, it was a sadness for this particular cow. One that had contracted a disease through no fault of her own.

She had the misfortune of standing next to a tainted cow. Eating some hay with a bit of bodily fluid on it.

Now she carried a disease that would be her undoing.

Had been branded twice. Would no doubt be poked and prodded in the coming days for the absolution of his client.

"Sorry, old girl," Drake said. Hooked his arm around her neck. Gave her a little squeeze.

She seemed to sense the thoughts pouring out of him. Understand what he was trying to say. Nuzzled back against him.

Blew out a hot breath of air.

Together they crested the ridge they were on. Looked down through a sloping meadow. Saw his truck and Rink's. The barn.

Everything illuminated by the flashing red and blue strobes of a Sheriff's Department cruiser. Around them, a handful of shadows moved back and forth.

Drake kept one arm around the cow. Led her toward the cluster. Let her stop as often as she wanted to.

The walk in total took 45 minutes. By the time Drake arrived, his fingers were numb. His face was prickling with sensation.

Seven shadows stood in the headlights of the automobiles waiting for him. As he got closer, Drake recognized Sara and Rink, the Crew.

Picked out Kellogg and Sheriff Pratt.

Neither looked pleased to be there.

"What the hell is this all about?" Pratt asked as he approached. Anger in his voice. "We got a call for an emergency out here. So far all I've seen is a bunch of kids and a cow."

Drake bristled slightly at the use of the word *kid*. Unhooked his arm from around the cow. Led her over toward his truck.

"Kade, can you give us some light?"

Kade nodded. Wrenched open the driver's side door. Flipped on the headlights.

Harsh fluorescent beams shot out from the truck in a wide cone. The effect was blinding at first. Caused Drake to raise a hand to shield his eyes.

The cow to pull a bit against the rope.

"Easy girl, it's alright," Drake said. Turned her around so her left haunch stood perpendicular to the truck.

"Sheriff, this is why we called you," Drake said.

He had seen the brand only once himself. Just for a moment before beginning the long trek back.

One quick look was all that was needed.

Still glaring at everyone, Pratt stepped up into the light. Kellogg followed a pace behind.

"Somebody better start making sense soon," Pratt grumbled. "Or I'm taking you all into custody."

Drake waited as they approached. Turned on his flashlight to add extra wattage to the brand splashed across the cow's haunch.

"Actually Sheriff, I think tonight you'll be letting someone out of custody."

The Sheriff paused a moment. Looked up from beneath the brim of his hat at Drake. Let his distaste flow through an elongated stare.

Waited a full minute before shifting his gaze to the cow before him.

Drake watched as the Sheriff reacted exactly the way he hoped he would.

Exactly the way he had less than an hour before.

Behind him, all five of his friends leaned in. Peered at the same thing as the Sheriff.

Nobody made a sound.

"Is that...?" the Sheriff sputtered.

"Brand tampering," Drake said. Shot a finger out and outlined the letters TR. "Pretty damn obvious this cow is property of the Tierney Ranch."

Moved his hand down, traced the new WB laid over them. "And was made to look like it belonged to the Webb's."

Drake stepped back. Watched as Pratt reached out. Traced the same exact pattern he had. Leaned back.

Even in the artificial light, Drake could see how pale he was. Could almost hear his teeth chattering.

Something told him it had nothing to do with the cold.

"As you can see," Drake said. "The actions of Lukas Webb were not attempted murder. They were to point out what was really going on. Nothing more."

Pratt stood to full height. Shook his head.

"He still discharged a weapon in a public place."

"Which is a misdemeanor," Drake said. "You've had him in custody 10 hours now. That's pretty standard.

"Besides, he's in a hospital bed. Where's he going to go?"

Pratt worked his jaw up and down again. No sound came out.

"This is the exact same brand and pattern you'll find on the two cows that tested positive from the Webb Ranch. You can get official copies of the photos from the Department of Ag in Helena.

"Something tells me if you test this cow, she'll come back positive for brucellosis as well."

"Our cows are clean," Sara said. Turned everyone's attention her way. "Papa always insisted on it."

"Simple fact is, Holt Tierney wanted their land," Drake said. "When they wouldn't sell, he tried to run them out by tainting their herd."

Pratt glanced around the group. Shook his head.

"You realize-"

"That you need to leave us here and go arrest Holt Tierney?" Drake finished. "Yeah, we know."

From the corner of his eye, he could see Sage smile. Ajax look away.

Pratt pulled his hat back away from his head.

"You know I can't just release Lukas tonight."

Drake nodded in concession. He'd been expecting that.

"I'll talk to Paula Goslin in the morning, get the charges formally dropped. Like I said, until then, it's not like he's going anywhere."

Pratt cast a look around the group. Ran a hand back over his hair. Turned to Kellogg.

"Andy, do something about this cow will you? It just became evidence."

Kellogg's jaw dropped open. He stood rooted in place as Pratt walked toward his cruiser. Opened the door.

"Uh, like what, exactly, sir?" Kellogg asked.

"Hell if I know," Pratt said. "I have to go find Holt Tierney."

CHAPTER FORTY-FIVE

Caravan.

Three trucks. Nose to tail. Right through the center of town.

Rink and Sara in the lead. Going first so Sara could direct them where to go.

Drake and Sage behind them. Riding close.

Kade and Ajax bringing up the rear.

No more than a few minutes passed after Sheriff Pratt left before something clicked in the back of Drake's mind. Remembered the newspaper article he'd read days before. Asked Sage for confirmation.

Tonight was the night of the Winter Ball.

Holt Tierney's very own showcase for all of Ravalli County.

Everybody was welcome. A night of well-intentioned fun and frivolity.

Charged with the prospect of seeing Holt Tierney's public downfall, the group moved into action. Corralled the cow into the back corner of the barn. Got it set up with plenty of alfalfa and water for the night.

Had Deputy Kellogg take photos in the off-chance somebody tried something before morning.

The second the *evidence* was secure, they piled into the trucks. Ignored their odd attire. The aching cold. Their complete lack of sleep.

Drove three-deep in a line across town. Rolled through the deserted square. Headed toward the Tierney Ranch.

All of them went a little faster than necessary.

None of them cared.

As they drove, Drake extended an arm along the back of the bench seat. Clasped Sage on the shoulder. Gave it a squeeze.

"You doing okay over there?"

Felt her hair whip across his knuckles as she turned to face him.

"I'm good," she said. Flashed her teeth at him in the darkness.

"Listen, I'm really sorry about-"

"Don't," Sage said. Lowered her cheek against her hand. "You don't have to do that with me. I'm not Ava."

The comment drew a laugh from Drake. A second squeeze.

"No, you definitely are not."

Ahead in the darkness, the main hall of the Tierney Ranch was lit up like a Christmas Tree. Originally a barn, it had long since been converted into an entertainment hub.

Tonight, it threw light in every direction. Shined like a beacon through the cold Montana evening.

"Not one for modesty, is he?" Drake asked. Alternated glances between the barn and Rink's bumper in front of him.

"Kind of makes you wonder what he's compensating for, doesn't it?" Sage added.

"I'd rather not," Drake replied. Followed Rink into the parking lot. Slid to a stop at an angle less than 30 feet from the front door.

Disregarded the even rows of parked cars.

Handfuls of people stopped what they were doing as the six piled out. Looked them up and down in their ski clothes and boots.

Some of the women laughed. A few of the men sneered.

The Crew ignored them all.

Bright light pushed its way out through every window in the barn. Through the glass doors on each side.

Greenery with red bows decorated the outer walls, twinkled with white lights.

The sound of a band could be heard carrying through the air. The din of voices in conversation.

The smell of food.

"How do you want to handle this?" Rink asked. Stopped and waited for the group to gather in.

"Sara?" Drake asked.

She shook her head. Pointed a bony index finger toward him. "You're doing great. Go ahead and finish it."

Drake ignored the compliment. Leaned back and looked the length of the barn.

Put together a rough plan in his head.

"I don't see Pratt's cruiser or any flashing lights yet, so I'm guessing he's not here. Has to be just a matter of time though, right?"

Several heads nodded.

"That's what the man said," Ajax added.

"So the question is, do we wait for him? Or go mess with Tierney a little bit first?"

Drake looked around the group.

Sara stared back at him. Rink scowled. The rest of the Crew wore mischievous grins.

The same smile grew on his face.

"Yeah, that's what I thought." Leaned in close. "Alright, Sara, you stay here with me. We'll give each of the other four a minute to get into place. Then we'll go in.

"The rest of you take an exit. Make sure he sees you. Knows he's not going anywhere."

Kade and Ajax nodded. Moved off for the far doors.

Rink squeezed Sara on the shoulder. Headed for the opposite side.

Sage waited an extra moment. Walked three across with Drake and Sara through the front.

Together they walked inside to a party long in-progress.

The enormous barn sprawled out in front of them. Roughhewn wood. Exposed beams. Wrought iron chandeliers.

Casual elegance.

Christmas trees lined the walls. A brass band played on a stage along the back wall. Round tables encircled a parquet dance floor.

Food and drink took up one entire side of the room.

A menagerie of sound and smell hit as they entered. A few people turned to examine them. Looked away just as fast.

"Alright, make us proud," Sage said. Fell back. Waited by the door.

Drake reached up and patted Sara on the back. Took a deep breath.

Spotted Tierney talking to an older couple just off the edge of the dance floor.

"You ready?" Drake asked. Started walking. Looked over to make sure Sara was doing the same.

Sara ignored the question. Stared at her surroundings.

"I had no idea this even existed. Must be over half the town."

Drake examined the crowd. Noticed most of them were older. Well-dressed. Giving he and Sara sideways glances.

"Yeah, but which half?" Drake asked.

Sara nodded. Followed Drake's lead as they cut a path through the crowd.

Tierney spotted them as they came closer. Did his best to keep the smile he was wearing in place. Glanced between the couple he was talking to and them as they approached.

Drake made no effort to let him finish his conversation. Had no desire to let him save any face.

Wanted every last person in Hamilton, in Montana, to know what he'd done.

"Holt Tierney," Drake said. Voice sharp. Loud enough that several heads turned to face him.

Felt Sara press in tighter by his side.

For his part, Tierney tried his best to look surprised. Raised his chin and eyebrows while being addressed.

"Mr. Bell, Ms. Webb, so nice of you to join us. I'm so glad to see you didn't let a little thing like a dress code stop you from coming out to have a good time."

Drake lowered his chin toward Sara. Kept his gaze on Tierney.

"This is going to be downright fun, you know it?"

"Agreed," Sara said. Focused her stare on Tierney.

The faux smile faded from Tierney's features. He shifted his attention to the couple beside him.

"Fran? Bruce? Would you mind excusing us for a moment?"

Drake held out a hand. Spread his fingers wide.

"Oh no, please, Fran and Bruce, stay. This will only take a minute.

"See, Holt, the reason we're dressed like this is we've spent all evening out in the Webb's pasture. Care to guess what we found out there?"

The color drained from Tierney's face. Any sort of expression soon followed. His features hardened.

"Judging by the smell, I'd say manure."

Drake snorted. Rolled his eyes.

"True. We also found ourselves a cow. One very interesting cow. One that was wearing your brand, changed to look like the Webb brand."

Fran and Bruce stood silent. Looked at Drake and back to their host.

Tierney met their glance.

"That's absurd. I'm quite certain I have no idea what you're talking about."

"It's also the same brand they found on two cows that tested positive for brucellosis this week," Drake said. "Wouldn't happen to know anything about that, would you?"

Tierney glanced around. Made an overhead motion with his hand.

A pair of men emerged from behind the bar. Thick, dressed in jeans and vests, they started across the dance floor.

"Oh, I don't think you want to do that either, Holt," Drake said. "If you look right now, you'll see a few people dressed like us standing by each of your exits.

"And trust me, you don't want to see them mad."

"I bet he wouldn't want us to start raising our voices either," Sara said. Tone louder by several decibels. Venom dripping from the words. "Tell the whole town how he tried to steal my family's ranch by framing us with brucellosis."

Several more heads turned. Conversations ceased.

"Now then, young lady, I don't know what it is you think you know, but you can't come in here making these kinds of accusations."

"Kiss my ass," Sara said. "I wish Lukas had shot more than just your picture."

Fran gasped. Reached out and grasped her husband's forearm.

A reflexive grin creased Drake's face.

"Alright, I think that's about enough of that," Tierney said. "Gentlemen, please escort these two out."

Drake looked at them edging closer. Almost dared them to try and lead him away.

Knew that Rink had been a coiled ball of fury all week. Shuddered at what his friend would do to them if they came near Sara.

Didn't have the chance to see how it played out.

Saw Sheriff Pratt enter through the side door. Walk past Kade and out into the middle of the dance floor.

Walsh on one side. LeGrange on the other.

An expression in place that showed he'd rather be any place else in the world.

"No need, gentlemen," Drake said to the hired hands. Motioned at Pratt and his deputies approaching. "We were all just leaving, weren't we Holt?"

Tierney's jaw dropped open. He glanced toward the other exits.

Saw Rink, Ajax, Sage, walking forward.

Drake watched Tierney glance from door to door. Could see him trying to figure out his next step. Determine what to do.

Almost smiled as the old man stood rooted in place. Nowhere to go. Frozen stiff, no ability to move if there was.

In the back of the room, the band ceased playing. People stopped dancing. Conversations died off.

The only sound was Pratt and his men walking out across the floor.

Drake stood a moment longer. Put a hand around Sara's shoulder. Turned them both back toward the door.

"Come on Sara, I think our job here is done. Let's go see how Lukas is doing."

CHAPTER FORTY-SIX

Forty-One.

Drake made it 41 hours before collapsing into bed on Saturday night.

Didn't remember climbing out of the three layers of clothes that encased him. Didn't recall Suzy Q curling up against his hip.

Didn't even register that he had set his alarm clock for 8:00 the next morning.

The moment it went off, his reaction was somewhere between relief and disgust. He was glad he had set it. Needed to be in Hamilton by 10:00.

Was flat angry he had set the meeting the night before for so early. Wondered what in the world he was thinking as he showered. Dressed.

Made one final trip down through the valley.

The parking lot of the Ravalli County Courthouse was deserted when Drake pulled up, save a lone vehicle.

An oversized, metallic blue Chevy Silverado.

When Drake spotted her on his way out of the Winter Ball and told her they needed to meet, he had offered to hold it in the Hamilton Memorial cafeteria again.

Even hinted that since she seemed to enjoy being seen there so much, he would be happy to do so.

The comment was not well received.

The request to meet was not either. Would have been pushed aside until Sheriff Pratt suggested it would be a good idea.

Was still balked at until Judge Ramey overheard and said he thought so as well.

There was no way to stop the smile from forming on Drake's face as he swung out of the truck. Headed in through the side door of the courthouse toward the Ravalli County Attorney's Office.

Less than half of the lights were on in the building as he walked through. The sound of his shoes echoed through empty rooms.

The air was chilly, the heat turned down for the long holiday weekend.

Drake followed a sparse path of overhead lights to the back corner of the office. Found Goslin seated behind her desk. Jeans and an oversized sweater. Hair pinned back. No makeup.

The ensemble made Drake shudder to think of how she would look the next morning, after New Year's Eve.

She looked up as he entered. Set aside a piece of paper. Gave him an icy stare.

"Good morning," Drake said. Stepped inside.

"Good morning," Goslin echoed. Motioned for him to sit.

Drake did so. Kept his jacket on. Laced his fingers in his lap.

"Thank you for meeting me here," Drake said. "I know this wasn't your idea."

As much as every fiber in his being wanted to gloat, he couldn't let himself. There was no way to know when or if his path may cross with her again.

Maybe even worse, if the Webbs might encounter her again.

"No," Goslin said. Voice frigid. "But we're here, so let's get on with it."

Drake pressed his lips together. Nodded. "Okay, obviously I'm here to see that all charges are dropped against Lukas Webb. That means he is no longer in custody and his record is wiped clean."

Goslin arched an eyebrow. Stared at him.

"He walked into a public gathering and fired a weapon. I can reduce charges, but I'm not dropping everything."

For a moment, Drake considered pointing out that she had omitted the words "peaceably" and "assault" from the canned speech she'd been giving reporters all week.

Opted against it.

"We both know public discharge is a misdemeanor. He already served the better part of a day in custody."

"For which he laid in a hospital bed," Goslin retorted.

"Irrelevant," Drake replied. "Besides, is that really much different from the holding cell at the other end of the hall here?"

"Community service," Goslin said. "And the incident stays on his record."

"I'd say the man's served enough, wouldn't you?" Drake said.

Silence fell.

Goslin leaned forward. Folded her hands in front of her. Stared across at Drake.

Or, more aptly, glared.

"Let's cut to the chase here, Mr. Bell. How would you like this to end?"

It was the question Drake half-expected her to open with. The fact that she'd gone through the charade as long as she did was a testament to her doggedness as a County Attorney.

"Last night, you were handed a much, much bigger prize than Lukas Webb," Drake said. "You got two press conferences out of the shooting. Imagine what you can milk this thing for."

Goslin drew her mouth into a line so tight her lips almost disappeared.

"I'm not going to let him go without *something*. At the very least, an either/or."

Drake nodded. There was no way he would accept jail time, a fine, or anything that stayed on a permanent record.

Otherwise, provided there an easy enough either/or clause attached, he could live with it.

Figured Lukas could as well.

"Alright, what do you propose?" Drake asked.

CHAPTER FORTY-SEVEN

Seahawks. Niners.

Rink and Lukas were both watching the game as Drake entered. Sara sat between them, dozing in a chair.

"Happy New Year," Drake said. Walked in. Fell back into a chair at the end of the bed.

Lukas and Rink both nodded in greeting.

"Happy New Year," Sara managed. Voice thick with sleep.

"I don't know about happy," Lukas said, "but a hell of a lot better than a day or two ago."

"True," Drake conceded. Raised his eyebrows. Nodded. "Sorry to drop by unannounced like this and ruin your first Sunday of football watching in what must have been quite a while."

"Eh," Lukas said. Waved a hand at the screen. "Last week of the regular season is terrible. Like watching preseason."

Drake turned over a shoulder. Glanced up at the screen.

"Yeah, both of these teams are already in the playoffs. They're not about to play their starters."

"Still better than watching the Broncos on the other channel," Rink said.

Drew chuckles from Drake and Lukas both.

"So, the reason I swung through was to tell you I spoke with Paula Goslin this morning."

Sara sat up in her chair. Rubbed her eyes.

"And?"

"And she's agreed to drop all charges." He paused. Held up a finger. Smiled. "Provided you agree to take a firearms safety course."

Slow smiles spread on the faces of all three.

Nobody spoke for a moment, unsure if he was joking.

Drake's own smile grew larger. "I'm 100% serious. I refused any fines or community service. She wouldn't let it go without something."

Sara was the first to crack. Let out an elongated sigh of surprise.

Rink shook his head. Grinned.

"So that *something* was to have a trained Army sniper take a firearm safety course?" Lukas said. Eyes bulged in disbelief.

"That's what I said," Drake replied. "I told her you could teach the damn thing, but she insisted."

Lukas raised his palms to his eyes. Pressed down on them.

"And if I don't?"

"If you don't, then it could escalate," Drake said. "Goes back to being a misdemeanor on your record."

"So I have to go," Lukas said. Not a question.

"You don't have to," Drake said. "But it's in your best interest."

"Anything else?" Rink asked.

"Not for us. I asked her what she was going to go after Tierney for, kind of not-so-subtly reminded her that she was pursuing the maximum penalty against Lukas just a couple of days ago.

"She picked up on the insinuation. Was not happy about it, but shared with me that she intends to go after Tierney too.

"Fraud. Trespass. Destruction of property. Conspiracy to commit murder. Rather lengthy list. Should get him a nice long stay up in Deer Lodge."

"Oh, they'll love him there," Sara said. Rolled her eyes.

"Even more so if they knew what he was in for," Rink said. Weighed the statement. "I'll see what I can do."

Drew a trio of uncertain laughs, nobody quite sure if he was serious or not.

"How are you feeling?" Drake asked. Obvious change of subject.

"Getting better," Lukas replied. "The fog has lifted a little more. Doc says I can go home middle of the week."

"Good," Drake said. Paused a moment. Clapped his hands in front of him. Stood.

"Hold on, you don't have to run off so soon," Sara said. "We're just hanging out here. Welcome to stay."

"I would love to," Drake said. "But I let my friends talk me into joining them out for New Year's Eve tonight. If I don't get home and get some more sleep, I won't see 9:00, let alone midnight."

From his perch in the bed, Lukas leaned forward. Extended a hand.

"Thank you, for everything. Seriously. You didn't know me from Adam, and really stuck your neck out for me. I won't forget it."

Drake returned the handshake. Nodded.

"You're welcome."

Lukas stared hard at him. No trace of mirth in his eyes.

"I'm not just paying lip service here. If you ever need anything, I'm your guy."

"Thank you," Drake said. "I appreciate that."

Released the handshake. Paused as Sara stood and gave him a hug. Kissed him on the cheek. Thanked him as well.

The final person was Rink, who stood. Shook his hand. Promised to stop by his house the next day.

Drake knew what it meant. Wanted to tell him it was unnecessary.

Wouldn't dream of doing it in front of the Webbs.

He made it as far as the door before remembering one last thing from his conversation with Goslin. Turned. Leaned a shoulder against the door frame.

"Oh, and I almost forgot. Based on a suggestion from General Hall, I kind of let it be known that the veterans of Ravalli County didn't appreciate Goslin's little speech the other day.

"I'd expect a nice donation to be made to the Amvets in your name before the end of the week."

EPILOGUE

"Eight days!"

Clear exasperation. Disbelief.

"I'm gone eight damn days and you manage to get yourself in trouble again?" Ava exclaimed.

Drake held the phone a few inches away from his face. Smiled. Shook his head.

"Come on, it wasn't quite like that. I didn't get in trouble, I just had a case randomly come up."

"I'm sorry," Ava said. Let her disapproval pour through the phone line. "Did you or did not say at one point you were staring at a gun?"

Drake sighed. "Remind me why I called to wish you a Happy New Year again?"

"You didn't," Ava replied. "I called you."

"Oh, yeah," Drake conceded. "Sorry, I've been off the grid the last week or so."

"Oh, yeah, I noticed," Ava said. Mocked his tone.

Drake smiled. Set his fingers into Q's ribs as she pressed against his side. Scratched.

The effort earned him a pair of opened eyes. A glance up from her spot beside him.

"Big plans for the evening?" Drake asked.

"Family," Ava said. "You'd think I'd been lost on a desert island the last three months or something the way they're acting. I'm so damn sick of family I'm actually kind of missing Montana at the moment."

"Ha!" Drake coughed out. Made no effort to mask his chuckles. Rolled over onto his side. "Now there's something I never thought I'd hear."

"Yeah, yeah. So how about you? Crazy night on the couch?"

The comment stung just a bit. For a moment Drake considered firing back a retort.

Stopped, realizing she wasn't entirely incorrect.

"Actually, the Crew is headed downtown. To do what, I'm not sure, but I'm guessing a good story or two will come from it."

"Try not to let that story involve a gun this time, huh?"

Drake smiled. Signed off the call a moment later. Dressed into jeans and a black pullover. Walked into the living room to find Ajax watching football, waiting for him.

A sour look on his face.

"You finally get done in there?" Ajax asked. Watched as a Clemson receiver broke a run down the sideline. Was pushed out of bounds just short of a touchdown.

Drake looked down at the phone in his hand. Checked the time.

"What? I was in there like 10 minutes."

"More like 30," Ajax said. "Cackling the whole time, too. Sounded like my mother with her friends at church."

Drake rolled his eyes. Headed for the door.

Ajax pulled on his heavy winter coat. Followed him out to the truck.

Despite it being New Year's Eve, the streets were still almost empty as they drove into town. Holiday or not, a college town without students is a barren place.

And there was no doubt that Missoula was a college town.

Drake pulled into a diagonal parking spot in front of Blue's six minutes after their agreed-to meeting time. Checked the clock on the dash. Stared through the windshield.

A low-slung building looked back at them. Neon signs beckoned. Extolled most every type of beer known to man.

"Remind me, is this the final destination or the first of many?" Drake asked.

"You wish," Ajax said. Pulled on the door handle. "Kade has set up a night of golf for us."

Drake climbed out the other side. Met Ajax in front of the truck. Walked toward the front door.

"Golf?" Drake asked.

"Yup. Nine watering holes in one night."

"Heaven help us," Drake muttered. Followed Ajax inside. Nodded to a Griz football player working the door.

Inside, the place looked exactly as the outside indicated.

Sports memorabilia from local teams covered the walls. A bar extended the entire right end. A bank of televisions above it played college football and professional basketball games.

Slot machines extended along the back.

Neon light bathed everything in a shade of reddish-green.

A shrill whistle went up from the corner. Drake and Ajax turned to see Kade and Sage seated at a round table.

A pitcher of beer sat in front of them, already half gone.

No question who was responsible for most of it.

Weaving through the crowd, they came upon the table together. Pulled up chairs on the end, backs to the room.

"You guys started without us?" Ajax asked. Went straight for a glass. Helped himself to some Moose Drool.

Kade took a long pull off his beer. Smacked his lips. Held the glass out toward them.

"Hey, you guys were late. I told you we're on a tight schedule tonight."

Ajax took a matching drink. Tossed the top of his head toward Drake.

"Talk to Chatterbox over here. Couldn't get him out the door."

Kade made a face. Set his beer down.

"Drake Bell talked on the phone? For longer than a minute? I didn't think he knew how to do that."

"Apparently, he does when Ava calls," Ajax said. Took another drink.

Drake rolled his eyes. Ignored the look from Kade. Glanced at Sage.

"Please let the record show that only one of us had to have their mama *buy* them female companionship this holiday season."

Sage's face cracked into a smile. Beside her, Kade almost spit out his beer.

All three shook with laughter as Ajax sat stoic. Raised his beer to his lips. Took a pull.

"All of you can go to Hell," he said. Kept his face impassive.

Did his best to convey that he actually meant it.

"Alright," Kade said. Leaned forward. Rested an elbow on the table. Extended his hand toward Drake.

"While hilarious, right now the more pressing question is not about Ajax and the prostitute his parents got for him."

"Man, she was not a prostitute!" Ajax snapped. "The girl has a master's from Boston College for crying out loud."

"Oh, I'm sure she's mastered a few things," Drake quipped. Earned another grin from Sage.

"Again," Kade said. Raised his voice a bit higher. "While hilarious, this is not about Ajax right now.

"Mr. Bell, is there anything going on with Ava?"

Drake made a face. Leaned back a bit.

"What? Of course not. She just called to say Happy New Year. To all of us."

He added the last line for Sage's benefit. Glanced her way as he said it.

"Okay," Kade said. "So then let me ask you this, of all the ladies that have been in your life, is there any you would say you have missed at all?"

"Maggie Grace," Drake said. No delay. No irony at all in his tone.

"Maggie Grace?" Sage asked. "Isn't that the actress from *Lost*."

"The smoking hot actress from *Lost*," Ajax corrected.

"No, I'm being serious," Kade pressed. "What woman *that you actually had a chance with* have you ever wished you could see again?"

"Maggie Grace," Drake repeated. Got chuckles from Sage and Ajax.

An exasperated look from Kade.

"Why do you ask?" Drake said. Shook his head. "And why am I on the hot seat here?"

Kade motioned toward the bar with his chin. "Because your back's to the room and you can't see who just walked in here."

Drake's mouth formed into a circle. He started to ask who. Stopped himself. Glanced over his shoulder.

Picked her out the moment he turned.

Same long brown curls. Full lips. Sea green eyes.

"Who just walked in here?" Sage asked. Rose an inch or two out of her seat to look.

Drake turned back to face the table.

"Emily."

Kade and Ajax both fell silent.

Sage's eyes grew large. "You mean *Emily* Emily?"

"Uh-huh," Kade said.

"The proverbial One That Got Away," Ajax added.

Drake ignored them all. Stared down at the table.

Said nothing.

———

Turn the page for a sneak peek of *The Glue Guy*, A Zoo Crew Novel book 4.

SNEAK PEEK

The Glue Guy, A Zoo Crew Novel Book 4

Chapter One:

Fog.

Condensation.

Every few moments, Dale Garvey reached out and smeared it away from the front windshield. Left wet circles across the inside of the glass. Wiped his hand along the leg of his jeans.

"You know that leaves marks on your windshield," Megan Rayner said from the passenger seat.

Sliding his eyes shut, Garvey pushed a loud breath out through his nose. Made sure she heard it. Opened his eyes again without looking over. In the darkened interior of the truck, he would barely be able to see her.

Wasn't sure he wanted to anyway.

If not for the fact that he couldn't do what he had set out to alone, he would have left her at home. She wasn't yet ready for this. Hadn't been through what he had.

But there was nobody else.

"I know," he said. Still didn't bother to look over at her. "But I can't risk turning the engine on to run the defrost."

Together, the pair had been seated in the darkness for over two hours. Despite the steadily dropping temperatures in the interior of the truck, there was still no way to keep the windows from fogging over.

From Garvey having to wipe them clean every so often.

"Are you sure about this?" Megan asked.

It was the fifth time since they'd parked that she'd asked the question. Each time she did, it raised the annoyance within Garvey a little higher.

Just beneath the surface, he could feel it lurking. Building. Waiting to explode.

Once more he drew in a deep breath. Willed himself to remain calm.

He couldn't do this alone.

"Yes," Garvey said. Forced his voice somewhere close to neutral. "You saw what's happening down there. It's only going to get worse. We can't allow that."

A moment of silence passed. Garvey hoped it meant she was finally accepting his explanation.

Knew better than to actually believe it.

"And you think this is the best way to ensure that?"

It was the first time a question had been posed without direct opposition. An inquiry asking for his thoughts. Nothing more.

Seated behind the wheel of his truck, Garvey felt the corners of his mouth rise.

She was coming around. Just as she always did.

"Of course," he said. Lowered his voice into something resembling a soothing tone. "That's why we're sitting out here in the cold right now. We don't actually want to hurt anybody, we just need to make sure we're taken seriously."

Beside him he could hear Megan sniffle. Whether it was from the frigid interior of the truck or stifled crying he couldn't be sure.

"Okay," she whispered. "I just want to make sure we don't hurt anybody."

"Never," Garvey said. Reached a hand out along the back of the bench seat. Slid his fingers in behind her long brown hair. Massaged her neck.

For a moment, her entire body was rigid. Seemed to resist his touch.

After a few seconds, the tension released. She leaned back into the steady kneading of his fingers. Let out the slightest moan of pleasure.

Having to pacify her trepidations was fast becoming a nuisance. She wasn't made from the same stuff as him. Didn't have the same convictions. For the time being though, that didn't matter. He didn't need her to believe in the cause, he needed her to believe in him.

As far as his purposes now required, that was enough.

Garvey kept his hand in place and turned his focus back out through the window. Stared through the circle already beginning to fog over again.

Felt his adrenaline spike as a pair of headlights appeared in the distance.

There was no chance they could be seen from where they were parked. The pull-off was too remote, the color of the truck too dark for that.

The jolt of electricity shooting through him was rather a result of what the headlights symbolized.

Six times in the preceding weeks, Garvey had staked out the place. Even managed to get inside once. He knew there was no set schedule to when the maintenance man came and went. Just that he seemed to arrive sometime after ten. Depart late in the evening.

The important thing was that after he did, nobody else disturbed the house. The woman - the only other staff on site - hadn't been seen in some time.

The headlights meant they now had nothing but unimpeded access for eight solid hours.

Pulling his hand away, Garvey watched as the headlights disappeared in the distance. Glanced over his shoulder at the supplies piled high in the bed of the truck. At the green cylinder propped up on the seat between them, secured into place with a seat belt.

The most important item of the evening for their purposes.

Garvey reached out and turned over the ignition. Waited as it warmed and the first blast of hot air hit him in over two hours.

Once the glass was clear, he put the truck into gear and eased forward without turning on the lights.

The house was now empty.

It was time to move.

———

**Continue reading *The Glue Guy*, A Zoo Crew Novel book 4:
dustinstevens.com/GGwb**

THANK YOU

Thank you so much for taking the time to read my work. I know you have literally millions of options available when it comes to making Kindle purchases, and I truly appreciate you taking the time to select this novel. I hope you enjoyed it.

If you would be so inclined, I would greatly appreciate a review letting me know your thoughts on the work. Going against traditional writer protocol I look at all reviews, not in some form of misguided vanity but in hopes of producing a better product. I assure you I do take what is said to heart and am constantly trying to incorporate your suggestions.

In addition, as a token of my appreciation, please enjoy a free download of my novel *21 Hours*, available **HERE.**

Best,

FREE BOOK

Join my newsletter list, and receive a copy of 21 Hours—my original best-seller and still one of my personal favorites—as a welcome gift!

dustinstevens.com/free-book

DUSTIN'S BOOKS

Works Written by Dustin Stevens:

Reed & Billie Novels:
The Boat Man
The Good Son
The Kid
The Partnership
Justice
The Scorekeeper
The Bear
The Driver

Hawk Tate Novels:
Cold Fire
Cover Fire
Fire and Ice
Hellfire
Home Fire
Wild Fire

Zoo Crew Novels:
The Zoo Crew
Dead Peasants
Tracer
The Glue Guy
Moonblink
The Shuffle
Smoked
(Coming 2021)

Ham Novels:
HAM
EVEN
RULES
(Coming 2020)

My Mira Saga
Spare Change
Office Visit
Fair Trade
Ships Passing
Warning Shot
Battle Cry
(Coming 2020)
Steel Trap
(Coming 2021)

Standalone Thrillers:
Four
Ohana
Liberation Day
Twelve
21 Hours
Catastrophic
Scars and Stars
Motive

Going Viral
The Debt
One Last Day
The Subway
The Exchange
Shoot to Wound
Peeping Thoms
The Ring
Decisions

Standalone Dramas:
Just A Game
Be My Eyes
Quarterback

Children's Books w/ Maddie Stevens:
Danny the Daydreamer...Goes to the Grammy's
Danny the Daydreamer...Visits the Old West
Danny the Daydreamer...Goes to the Moon
(Coming Soon)

Works Written by T.R. Kohler:
The Hunter

ABOUT THE AUTHOR

Dustin Stevens is the author of more than 50 novels, the vast majority having become #1 Amazon bestsellers, including the Reed & Billie and Hawk Tate series. *The Boat Man*, the first release in the best-selling Reed & Billie series, was named the 2016 Indie Award winner for E-Book fiction. The freestanding work *The Debt* was named an Independent Author Network action/adventure novel of the year for 2017 and *The Exchange* was recognized for independent E-Book fiction in 2018.

He also writes thrillers and assorted other stories under the pseudonym T.R. Kohler.

A member of the Mystery Writers of America and Thriller Writers International, he resides in Honolulu, Hawaii.

Let's Keep in Touch:
Website: dustinstevens.com
Facebook: dustinstevens.com/fcbk
Twitter: dustinstevens.com/tw
Instagram: dustinstevens.com/DSinsta
Facebook Group: dustinstevens.com/RideAlong

CPSIA information can be obtained
at www.ICGtesting.com
Printed in the USA
LVHW080334220221
679575LV00001B/99